HOVER

Also by Melissa West

Gravity

HOVER

MELISSA WEST

Entangled Publishing, LLC
2614 South Timberline Road
Suite 109
Fort Collins, CO 80525
Visit our website at www.entangledpublishing.com.

Edited by Liz Pelletier
Cover design by Heather Howland

Ebook ISBN 978-1-62266-009-4
Print ISBN 978-1-62266-008-7

Manufactured in the United States of America

First Edition August 2013

For my husband, Jason, and my two beautiful daughters, Rylie and Lainey. I love you with all that I am. Thank you for making my life complete.

CHAPTER 1

"What is that?" I ask, pointing to a dark triangular building in the distance. My tone is formal, focused, just as it always is when we're discussing the city's breakdown.

Emmy shifts beside me. Emmy has been my sole healer at the Panacea, the Ancients' version of a hospital, for nearly a month now. She is more personable than the other healers, who often appear exhausted or angry. I've been trying for weeks to understand the need for healers beyond their ability to maintain life on the Ancients' planet, Loge. They cultivate the land, nourish it. On Earth we might have called them corporeal Mother Natures. But when it comes to Ancients needing healers, I'm at a loss. Ancients have xylem running within their bodies, similarly to how humans have water. Xylem itself has healing properties, so why the need for healers? Something doesn't add up, yet each time I press Emmy on it, she gives me a distant look and responds with short answers that give me next to no insight into anything beyond the fact that my questions make her uncomfortable. This one is no exception.

"That be the Vortex," Emmy finally says, her speech different than the other Ancients I've encountered. It's intentionally choppy, like she can't be bothered to use complete sentences. She washes her hands together nervously as though they were under a faucet of water and she wanted to make sure the soap touched every inch of flesh. "RESs train there."

I nod. I know very little about the RESs, beyond that RES is short for Republic Employed Spy, and that Jackson is one of them.

I think to the night he revealed himself to me in my room. I was petrified. I had lost my Taking patch moments before, breaking one of the only formal rules of the Ancient/human treaty. The Taking patch was a small silver eye covering, created by the Chemists on Earth, to not only block our vision, but immobilize us, while the Ancients came into our rooms at night to Take our antibodies so they could acclimate to Earth. We weren't allowed to see them, an act punishable by death, and there I was, my eyes closed tightly as I waited for my Ancient to come and offer up my punishment. Only the punishment never came. I opened my eyes to find Jackson Locke hovering above me. *Jackson Locke.* My greatest competition for top seed in Field Training. Everything became so hectic after that moment. He told me about our refusal to allow the Ancients to coexist with us, as promised in the treaty, that soon a war would begin. He begged me to help him stop it. Before I truly knew what I was getting myself into, before I even allowed myself a second to think it through, I had agreed. And now…here I am, half human, half Ancient. A girl lost among strangers, linked to the enemy. Though, now, I no longer consider them the enemy. Maybe I never did. Something has changed within me. I never would have imagined humankind could be as brutal as we became in those weeks leading up to the release of the neurotoxin. The cylinders of Ancient organs. The testing chambers full of dead Ancient children. And then once we had released the neurotoxin and poisoned our own people, the execution chambers built to disingrate our remains.

I have no idea what the Ancients stand for, what morals ground them or what passion propels them, but I now know that deep within the human concept is something dark, selfish, and completely willing to do whatever is necessary to support the idea of humanity. Because that's what it is, an idea. True humanity would never behave as we have behaved.

I glance over to Emmy, and then back to the triangular building. Each day we do this. She comes in with the intention of checking on me and stuffing me with these circular healing foods called bocas, but we always end up by the window, staring out over Triad, the largest city on Loge, while I ask question after question. I try my best to hide my true intent, but my efforts are futile. Emmy knows, what I'm sure most here know. I am not one of them. I do not trust them. And I will do whatever is necessary to protect the other humans from them. After all, it's all but my fault they are here. If I would have gone to Dad about Jackson, if I would have confided in him, none of this might have happened.

My mind drifts to the days that led up to the release of the neurotoxin, to Jackson and how uneasy he had become. Why didn't I see it? We had spent weeks together, growing closer with each passing day. An intensity had built between us, a dependency on the other, that was unlike anything I had ever experienced. It was as though we were the only two people who understood what was happening, and through each other, we found comfort. More than comfort. My chest tightens at the thought of his lips on mine, his body pressed so closely to mine I could feel his heart beating in rhythm with my own. But even after all that, I never pushed him for details. Instead, I stood by helplessly as our Chemists released a poisonous neurotoxin into Earth's atmosphere, killing thousands. Of course, they couldn't have known how many humans had been healed by

Ancients over the years, effectively exposing them to Ancient xylem—effectively turning them *into* Ancients. They couldn't have known. I couldn't have known. So why did I feel so guilty?

I didn't ask for any of this. I didn't ask for Jackson to seek me out for help. I didn't ask for him to heal me, turning *me* into an Ancient. And I certainly didn't ask him to bring me to Loge, which cemented my guilt in place. Because while I was here, healing, those I cared about were on Earth, abandoned.

The constant ache in me to hear their voices, their reassurances that they're okay, is enough to drive me insane.

The main door to the Vortex opens, and I crane my neck to get a glimpse inside. Two Ancients exit, but from this distance, I can't make out anything inside.

"Do you think the humans are in there, Emmy?"

She sighs. "I don't know, child. Not my matters."

"But have you seen any of them? I mean, surely some have come here for treatment, right?" I glance at her, hopeful.

She shakes her head, looking conflicted.

At this point, I have more questions than I can possibly hold within my useless brain, which brings me back to the Vortex, and my true intent on pressing Emmy to tell me everything she can about Triad—I have no idea where the other humans are being held.

"Emmy?"

She averts her eyes, and I feel a common frustration bubbling up within me. "Fine." She knows. She just refuses to tell me.

I've been at the Panacea for three weeks. Three weeks of tests and analysis and enough bocas to feed all of my hometown of Sydia, and still, I have yet to see a single human. Not injured in the Panacea. Not dancing in the fields that cradle the city like a blanket. None. Not one. Which means either Zeus is keeping them somewhere…or they're all dead.

I study the Vortex, its almost black exterior, and imagine it full of men and women training, like Jackson, to pretend to be human on Earth, to kill humans by Taking them to death. A shiver creeps down my back. That has to be where the humans are being held.

"Come child, eat." Emmy holds out a bowl of bocas, purple on the outside, sunshine yellow on the inside. They taste like oranges, but look like grapes. "Young-one be here soon for assignation. We need to get you ready."

The assignation. There are four sectors in Triad of which one can be assigned to work—the factories, the schools, the military, or the government. The healers on Loge possess the ability to cultivate the land and heal living creatures by zeroing in on the inner workings of the person, animal, or plant and "fixing" whatever isn't working just right. That ability also allows them to look at that living thing's purpose. So, the top healers in Triad conjure together with Zeus to give an analysis on all Ancients once the Ancient turns sixteen. This analysis is known as the assignation, and the results determine which of the four sectors of Triad the individual will work. Most everyone goes to the factories, but advance intellect can often sway an individual towards military or government, which are the sought after jobs in Triad. Emmy tells stories of her kids pretending to be RESs, running around in disguise. It's prestigious. A mark of honor.

And the very last thing I want to be here.

The RESs are responsible for the attacks on Earth that led to the release of the neurotoxin. We may have killed thousands of our people by releasing the neurotoxin, but they killed thousands just to prove they could. Becoming an RES would be the ultimate betrayal. But in the end, I'm not sure I'll have a choice. It will all come down to Zeus. And if I have learned anything in the three weeks that I have lived in Triad, it's that what Zeus wants, Zeus gets.

I can still hear Emmy's words, mere days after Jackson brought me here to save me from the neurotoxin that was poisoning me to death. "Not young-one," she had said. "Old-one." And I knew, the words pounding into my head like a migraine until one single name appeared—Zeus. Zeus wanted me to become an Ancient. The question is…why?

The curtains to my private room sway, and I wait anxiously for Jackson to enter but no one emerges. Jackson and Emmy have been the only two people that I've seen since coming here. Though, I really shouldn't call them people. They aren't, even if they look as human as I do. But that's not why I call them people. I call them that because it makes me feel like I'm not really on another planet, just another country, like any day I could hop a hovercraft and fly home.

I've realized it's familiarity that grounds us, and without it, the mind drifts into dangerous territory. I've only considered death once, when the nightmares mixed so thoroughly with my thoughts that all I wanted was a little relief. Now, I'm medicated with one of their concoctions to make sure I don't drift again. I hate what it does to me, the constant humming in my brain as though I can't be trusted to think or act by myself. Emmy says she'll take me off it soon. Every day she says it will be soon. I'm starting to wonder if *soon* means something different here.

Aside from Emmy, Jackson comes by every day—and every day I try my best to avoid talking to him. I think to how quickly I trusted him. I've thought it through a thousand times. Why? Was it that I felt like I knew him? Because I did in a way. I had known Jackson—or the Jackson I thought he was— since we were kids. Seeing someone year after year, growing up together, gives you a sense of comfort, like you're predisposed to trust simply because you remember what the person looked like six inches shorter. I don't know. Sometimes I think I'm just trying to make sense of my decisions, justify them, because the truth is, after weeks now of nothing but my own guilty thoughts, all I can come up with is hope.

The attacks were increasing. Everything felt so intense. I didn't need him to tell me that a war was coming—anyone with a brain could sense it. I needed to believe that we could stop it, that there was hope. And no one knows what it's like to trust on hope alone until they've been so deep in horror that there is nothing left *but* hope. That's where I was, maybe where I still am—in horror—but there is no worry of me trusting on hope again. I made that mistake once…and he let me down. Now I'm stuck here, waiting to learn what Zeus has planned for me.

"How you feel today, child?" Emmy asks after a while of silently staring down at Triad in motion. It's like watching clockwork move, everything and everyone so robotic I have to wonder if they are programmed.

"Good," I finally say and she smiles, taking my hand in hers. She has a youth about her, despite her outward appearance. Her hair is white, outside of an orphaned blonde strip in the front. Her face has creases around her eyes and mouth that suggest she's laughed more often than she's cried. I've never seen her laugh or even smile, which makes me wonder how long it's been since she felt the happiness that created her lines. She doesn't look at me, likely afraid I'll ask her, yet again, to explain what she had meant about Zeus. Questions about Triad she can handle, and does to appease me, but Zeus is another topic altogether.

I glance down at the bowl of bocas and prepare for how I'll ask her. "Emmy," I start.

She peeks behind her, making me wonder if Zeus's shadow follows her around. "I told you, no talk of him. Now, young-one be by soon. Eat. Food brings—"

"Healing. I know. Emmy, please…"

"Not my place. Now rest." She pats my hand one last time, leaning in to hug me, and says, "His eyes are everywhere here, his ears in the walls. Be careful, child." She straightens, pulls out the band of beads from her pocket that I've seen her reach for when she gets worried, and laces them through her fingers again and again, her look distant.

As soon as she leaves, I return my attention to the city. I find myself standing by my window for hours each day, surveying Triad, hoping to see something new that gives me an idea of where the humans are, but each day the sun sets with me knowing nothing more than I had learned the day before. Now, the sun rises from a wall of green foliage that lines the city, separating Triad from whatever lies beyond it. Within the wall, there are rows and rows of houses, neighborhoods perhaps. I imagine what they are doing in their homes. If they are eating dinner now or playing games or watching some version of a T-screen.

From the neighborhoods, a large bridge stretches over a river into a city that covers the rest of everything visible. Building after building, all with green roofs, all different sizes and as rustic looking as the Panacea. It's simple looking. But also beautiful, unlike anything I've ever seen before. Every day, I stare, mesmerized, until my eyes drift to the furthest edge of the city, to the rock-like building that stalks forever to the sky. There are no visible windows or doors in this building, giving it a look of complete power and terror. I remember asking Emmy what it was and her responding with only, "His." I didn't ask for clarification, I knew what she meant, and we ended up watching it together that day. Her eyes full of worry, mine of wonder.

I study Zeus's building now, watching for movement, when a loud scream from the hallway pierces the silence. My eyes snap to my doorway, my entire body suddenly on alert.

I start forward, eager to find out what caused it, when the curtain blocking my doorway bucks inward and a hand reaches inside, gone as quickly as it emerged, followed by another gut-wrenching scream.

I rush out into a long hallway. It's the same wood of my room, with five doorways lining each side. At the end of the hallway stand two Ancients carrying a girl who scrambles in their grasp to get away. She looks just like…

"Lexis?"

Her eyes find mine, her voice rich with fear. "Ari! Ari, please help me. *Help* me." She pushes out of their hold and is almost to me, when they jerk her back. "Don't let them take me back there. Please. I can't go back there."

I step forward, just as Emmy blocks my path. "No, stop, I know her," I say, panic rising up inside me as I take in Lexis's appearance. Her head has been shaved, her skin once a deep brown is now pale and dull. What have they done to her? "That's a girl from my school. Lexis. She isn't — "

"No, no, no," Lexis pleads as a lady approaches wearing the same shapeless green dress as Emmy and bearing what I can only imagine is a needle, but it isn't attached to a syringe and it's three times longer than any needle I've ever seen. At first I think she's going to use it as a weapon, and I try to push past Emmy, who seems to guess my moves before I make them, outmatching me with every step.

"Let me go," I shriek, growing angry and annoyed. The medication obviously hinders my reflexes as much as my emotions. "What is this? Why can't they leave her alone?"

Emmy eases me back, again shocking me with her strength and ability to move me without my realizing. "Quiet, child. Best turn an eye." She has me a foot from my room, when something catches my attention to the right. Another room, directly across from mine, the curtain open, exposing a person covered from neck to toe in an ivory wrap, her arms locked to her side. A gasp escapes my lips, and I push Emmy hard out of my way, torn between getting to the room or helping Lexis. I'm almost to the room, almost to Cybil, when one of the men who held Lexis locks his arms around me from behind, squeezing so hard I struggle to breathe.

"Release her," a voice growls, and everyone in the room freezes. The Ancient drops me hard to the ground, and I scramble up, astonished to see Jackson standing beside him. I didn't recognize his voice, so hard and authoritative, and now all I can do is watch him study the Ancient as though he's deciding whether to kill him immediately or torture him slowly. "This area is restricted. As you were informed."

"Yes, sir," the Ancient says. "The healers requested assistance with the human behind you. Then this one—"

"I did not ask for an explanation. You were informed. Exit now."

I peek around Jackson to an empty hall, Lexis now gone, and my eyes flash with fury. "Where did they take her? And what's wrong with Cybil?" I say to Jackson, ignoring Emmy's gasp at my tone.

Jackson hesitates, breathing in and out, calming himself with each release. "Let's go. We're now late for the assignation."

He leads me out the door at the end of the hall, down steps that seem to spiral forever, past an elderly Ancient at a large wooden desk, and then out an arched doorway and into the day. He never speaks the entire way, his jaw set so tightly I wonder if it's locked in place. As soon as we're a safe distance from the Panacea, I pull away from him. "What was that? What just happened back there?"

"I'm sorry," he says, as we step onto a pebble stone walkway lined with grass greener and thicker than anything we have back home. "You weren't supposed to see them like that. I know how it looks. Cybil is bad off. They've been working on her for days now with little to no change. The wrap is supposed to pull out impurities from her body. And Lexis…she's with some of the others who have been…difficult."

"What do you mean 'difficult'?"

"She's resisted treatment, resisted housing. At some point, we have to contain high risks like her to prevent our kind from singling them out. It's a safety measure."

I fight the urge to question his "safety measure," knowing I'm too clueless about what's happened to give a solid argument. All I know is that Lexis was petrified, and something about Jackson's excuse doesn't sound right. Either he doesn't have the full details or he's refusing to share them with me. I might have put up with his secrecy before, back when I was too concerned with losing everyone I loved to question him, but now, I have nothing to lose. I have no reason to hold back. So I turn on him, anger causing the veins in my head to pulse. "Enough with the shadowed talk. Tell me what's going on. Right now. Not later. Now." A hurt look crosses his face, and I have to glance away to maintain my anger. I hate looking at him like this, talking to him like this. I hate that it feels like we're on opposite sides. I want him on my side.

Jackson sighs, his face composed—patient—as though he's dealing with a crazy person and doesn't want to cause an episode. I guess he's not too far off. I feel crazy, but I'm telling myself it's the medication. "I'll do one better. I'll show you. But right now we're late."

All my anger from before vanishes, replaced by an immediate, more dominant feeling. Fear. I have never met Zeus before, even though he has been the Ancient leader since I was little, but I have seen him on the televised addresses with Earth's worldwide leaders. He has an eagle-like presence, his eyes always studying, his demeanor eerily calm.

We continue down the pathway in silence, my mind on Jackson and what we've become.

I think Jackson hoped I would forgive and forget, but I'm not wired that way. I can't just forget that he lied to me about his true identity. He could have told me, even if there was a good chance I would have turned him in the second I found out who he really was. Still…

His body tenses and he whips around, rage in his eyes. "You don't understand, okay? You don't know what I went through every single day that I couldn't tell you. You don't know how badly I wished everything were different. It isn't like—"

"What? Isn't like you lied intentionally? Does that even matter?" My own anger takes over. "I put everything on the line for you, gave you my complete trust. Why couldn't you do the same for me? This isn't as simple as you lying. You didn't trust me enough to tell me. And maybe you were right because there's a pretty good chance I would have shot you the moment you said you were Zeus's grandson!" The words come out so fast I can hardly register what I said, or that it's how I truly feel.

Jackson jerks back, his face painted first with hurt then anger. He nods and continues walking, leaving me standing on the path staring after him. I swallow hard, feeling a lump rising in my throat. I don't want to feel this way. I want to forgive him. I want to lean into him and feel his warmth settle over me like a blanket on a cold day.

But I can't.

CHAPTER 2

"This is our ride," Jackson says as I step up beside him, neither of us looking at the other. He points down to a river in front of us that ripples first blue then purple then crystal clear and back, like a fantasy. A single dark wooden raft with two large white sails awaits us. It's neither large nor small, able to hold maybe ten people.

Jackson takes my hand to help me aboard, and we both stiffen, electricity moving from his hand to mine. Heat rises up my neck, and for a moment, we're back in the woods behind my house, walking hand in hand, both of us unwilling to let go.

I release his hand the moment I'm on the boat, but I can still feel his touch long after his hand has left mine. I chance a look at the other Ancient and then to Jackson, who is watching me, his expression soft. He tilts his head, our eyes remaining locked, and though we are a few feet apart, it feels as though we are inches. Mere inches from breathing in the same air. Seeing him like this, it feels impossible that he's the same boy who lied to me, impossible even that he could be related to Zeus. But he is, he did, and I can't just forget. I'm not the kind of girl who just forgets.

I break contact and instantly my insides feel colder, sadder.

We drift down the river, the wind carrying us, it never seeming to die down, yet never causing me to feel chilled. I wonder what season we're in, if Loge even has seasons, and then I realize I'm thinking this nonsense to keep myself from panicking. I'm about to see Zeus, someone who evokes fear in everyone he meets, and I have no clue what to expect. I consider asking Jackson, but I'm afraid to question him in front of the other Ancient and after what I said I'm not sure he even wants to talk to me. Instead, I allow my gaze to take in this new world, studying as much of it as possible as we go.

The river separates the residential side of Triad from the city portion. We pass the rows of houses I saw at the Panacea, all tiny, squat things, each row with a different color roof. The last section we passed had red roofs. The one we're about to reach has yellow. I imagine it's a coding system, but of what I can't guess, because all the houses are exactly the same size, shape, everything—except the roof.

Jackson dips his head, biting back a smile. "Always curious."

"Not *always*. I'm— Hey, you're doing the sensing my thoughts thing. First back on the path, then here."

He nods. "Still an RES, so yeah. And trust me, with your thoughts today I wish I couldn't sense them."

I cringe. The RESs all have a device implanted into their hearing that detects stress levels and computes it into thoughts, allowing the Ancient to read the thoughts of others by reading his or her stress level. I start to reply, when he adds with a smirk, "Maybe try not to think so much." He fights to rein in his smile, then, losing the battle, bursts out laughing, the sound so pure I almost smile despite myself. "Never mind, that's impossible for you."

"Hey!" I jab him in the chest, and then a few things happen at once. The Ancient grabs me by the throat, lifting me into the air with one hand, while Jackson orders him to release me. The Ancient drops me hard against the edge of the boat, and I stumble back, unable to regain my balance, and splash into the river.

I expect to freeze on contact, but it's warm, like a bath, better than a bath. The boat stops beside me, and Jackson reaches out to help me back aboard. "I'm so sorry. Are you all right? He's taught to guard me. I'm sorry."

I push my soaked hair from my face. "It's fine. I'm fine."

He pulls me back into the boat, and I glance over at the Ancient to see a satisfied smile on his lips. It's then I realize he did it not because I jabbed Jackson, but to prove a point. To him, and to most here, I'm still human. I'm still an outsider.

"Sure you're okay?" Jackson asks.

"I'm fine," I say, tired already of having to maintain my anger at him. I've never been one to hold a grudge, something Gretchen and Law—my best friends from back home—have always joked about. They used to say I would make a terrible commander for no other reason than I'd forgive someone way faster than I'd shoot him. Of course, things have changed now.

Still…it doesn't help that I have more questions than my brain can hold. It would be so much easier if I could just shut off my anger, for at least a little while, so I could learn more about this place.

"You seem nervous."

"I am nervous. Can you blame me? I'm going to see the leader of Loge. It's a little daunting, though I'm sure you're used to him. After all, he's your grandfather."

Jackson looks away for several seconds, appearing to contemplate his words. "I know I should have told you. Danger or not, I should have said something. But I'm nothing like him, Ari." He takes a step toward me, his expression so full of emotion it takes my breath away. "Surely you know that. Surely you realize."

My eyes drop, unable to handle the overflow of feelings moving through me. "I don't know how I would have handled it, but still, I wish you would have told me. And about what I said before…I didn't mean…I shouldn't have…It's just a lot for me right now."

"It's okay." He rakes a hand through his hair, letting out a long breath as he steps back. "I know."

I clear my throat and stare out across the water.

"Can we…start over?" Jackson asks. "You need me here and I need you. I understand that you don't trust me right now. And clearly I didn't trust you enough either. So, let's start over."

I cock an eyebrow at him. "Why do you need me?"

"Most of my friends have no idea exactly what happened back on Earth, and some may not even care. I can't talk to them"—he glances up, his blond strands shadowing his eyes—"like I can talk to you. Or like I *could* talk to you. I don't want to lose that. We can try to be…friends."

The word twists in my mind uncomfortably. Friends. With Jackson. I think back to our first kiss, his fingertips on my face—my lips. I close my eyes to try to push the thought away and when I reopen them he's looking at me. "Okay," I say finally. "We'll be friends."

Before he can respond, we're interrupted by our arrival at the massive bridge. The Ancient anchors the boat and offers me a hand to exit, but Jackson pushes him away. "You're lucky I allowed you to ride the rest of the way with us instead of swim." I jump down onto a wooden walkway that curves up to the bridge and wait for Jackson to join me. His gaze drops to my clothes. "What are we going to do with you? You're soaked."

I glance down at my sopping wet shirt and laugh. "This should make a good impression."

"You can change. Come on." He points at one of the stores lining the street, all of them connected except the roofs. The wood of each building is stained a different color, this one the deep purplish blue of a blueberry, while others are red or orange or pink. He pulls me through the blue store's open doorway and into what looks like a clothing shop, but the clothes are…different. Sparkling rope drapes from wall to wall, all with different pieces hanging by color. A tiny Ancient with white blond hair stands as we edge further into the shop. She smiles at Jackson, but doesn't come over. Instead, she takes in my appearance and walks to a table in the front, grabs two garments, and hands them to me. "You can change in there." She nods toward a beaded curtain to my right that won't come close to hiding me from view.

"Thanks. But I don't have any way of paying you." I glance back to Jackson and then the girl, suddenly nervous. Do they even use currency here? Back home, they just scanned my keycard and then charged the bill to my parents. Though most never even scanned my card. With Dad as the Commander to the Engineers, they all knew who I was, so it wasn't necessary. Here, I have no idea how we buy things or what I would buy even if I did have some form of currency.

The girl smiles kindly. "You're covered."

Jackson shrugs. "Consider us even. You know, for the ice cream." His mouth twitches into an almost smile and for a second I want to smile back, and then I remember the rest of that afternoon. We had finished Operative training early and decided to go get ice cream in the Market District. We sat on a bench, and he talked to me forever about Loge—never once mentioning his true identity.

I look away. "Okay. I'll just…" I motion to the curtain and step behind it, wishing I could ask them both to turn around. I draw a breath and slip off my soaked clothes, sliding on the dry garments as quickly as I can. The shirt flows to my thighs, hanging off one shoulder and nothing more than a tank on the other. It's deep green and brown, with gold thread sewn in swirls here and there so the shirt looks almost exotic. Coupled with the skintight black pants she paired with it, I feel underdressed to be visiting Zeus, though I have a feeling my outfit is the least of my concerns.

I step out of the curtain, self-conscious. I wish Gretchen were here. Even on a different planet, she would know exactly how to dress. I remember her face just before Jackson brought me to Loge. She was kneeled in front of the Operatives, who were planning to kill her for aiding me in the release of the infected humans at the execution base. Lawrence was begging them to let her go. Cybil, my Operative trainer on Earth, was infected, like me, and she and I had devised a plan to attack on opposing sides, but then the injection Mom had given me to ward off the neurotoxin was wearing off. Everything went blurry. I could barely see. And then Jackson was in front of me, and when I woke, I was here, in Triad, everyone I loved a million stars away...

I feel a lump forming in my throat and swallow hard to release the pressure. "Is this okay?" I ask Jackson, gesturing to my clothes. His eyes slowly scan down my body, caressing each curve, before returning to my face. He shakes his head, says something I can't make out, then pushes out of the store, his arm outstretched for me to follow.

We walk down the main street of Triad in silence. It's an unusual city, though I suppose I haven't experienced many to know the difference. I had never traveled outside Sydia, the capital of America and my home, so maybe all cities look like this, though I doubt it. More shops decorate the streets—places to buy normal things like flowers, clothes, drinks, but also ivory, honey, and things I've never heard of before like arnica and gotu kola.

We reach the end of the street, and stop at Zeus's building. Etched into the front of the dark gray building is a single gold word—*Castello*. There are no guards at the entrance. No keycards. No security system. Back home, every building had a security system, but this, no doubt the most important building in all of Triad, is left unprotected. Somehow knowing this makes me more nervous, as though no one would be stupid enough to break into Zeus's building.

Inside, the building is all business—a set of what looks like elevators to the right, a swirling staircase to the left, and seated between the two is a male Ancient so huge he makes the guards from the Panacea look like children.

"Who is that?" I whisper to Jackson.

"One of Zeus's minions. Isn't that right, Ed?" Jackson asks, causing the guy to laugh in a way that says he could snap us in two if he wanted.

"You've got balls, J.C., I'll give you that. Is he expecting you?"

"J.C.?" I whisper. Oh, Jackson Castello, his true name as Zeus Castello's grandson.

Jackson smiles at the guard. "Isn't he always?"

He leads us to the swirling staircase, which is as dark and uninviting as the building itself. I clasp my hands together in front of me to keep them steady. I have no idea what will come from the assignation, but something tells me it isn't going to be all sunshine and flowers and hugs.

"Relax," Jackson whispers.

"I'm trying." And really I am, but being here, in Zeus's domain, has me on edge. At home I had a support system, people who had my back. It's easy to be brave when you know what you're getting into and whom you're getting into it with. Here, I know nothing and no one, which makes me wish I at least had a weapon on me.

Finally, after several long hallways and turns, we stop in front of a door with a guard stationed beside it. The guard, a tall male with long dark hair tied back, doesn't look at me, not even a quick glance.

"He's expecting us," Jackson says, his tone returning to the commanding one he used at the Panacea. The door opens inward into a grand room filled with thirty or so Ancients on the right and left. There is no sound inside the room, no talking, no shuffling of hands or feet. They watch us enter, some with looks of curiosity, others hatred.

My eyes travel to the front of the room where a long, ornate table seats two women and three men. One I recognize at once to be Zeus, and standing behind him with a devilish grin on her face is Mackenzie, the Ancient who was pretending to be Jackson's girlfriend back in Sydia. She and I were enemies from the beginning, but her animosity toward me elevated when Jackson and I grew close. He said she worked for his family. I guess that means she works for Zeus. Lovely. I'm sure *that's* going to work in my favor.

"Please, valued guests," Zeus says, "welcome Ari Alexander, our newest resident." His head twitches, then he blurts out, "Resident: a person who maintains domicile at a given place."

I watch him curiously, but no one else reacts to the recited definition. What is that about? A nervous tick or some strange thing he does to maintain internal peace?

His lips press together into a hard, disapproving line. "It's always refreshing to hear the judgmental idiosyncrasies of the human mind. For how different you pretend to be, on the inside you are all the same—small minded and closed off to anything different from the norm."

"Grandfather," Jackson says, a careful edge to his voice.

Zeus smiles. "Very well. We openly welcome you to Triad. Please know there are laws, as is required of any operating civilization. There are many, and while we do not pretend that you could memorize all, please note the following: honesty, magnanimity, and pride. These words, mere sentiments in your world, are the backbone of ours."

My jaw tightens. At some point, my over-opinionated head is going to blow. I have pride, loads of it—for *humans*. I glance nervously to Zeus, cursing myself for not controlling my thoughts better, but he doesn't respond. They can't expect me on the first day to toss aside my loyalties in favor of theirs.

This time Zeus refuses to remain silent. "You forget, you are no longer human. At least not fully. Testing revealed fifty-fifty. I suspect by yearend your body will have fully transformed. Before we begin, do you have any questions?"

An image of the T-screen back home filling with Zeus's face crosses my mind. We were shocked to hear his offer to allow all infected humans to come to Loge to be healed. At first, it seemed generous, *humane*, but now that I've spent time here, I know that nothing about Zeus is especially kind. I hold his gaze. "Yes. Where are the other humans?"

Jackson tenses noticeably beside me, but the question is already out and as stupid as it may be, I refuse to spend my time here afraid of Zeus. Besides, if he wanted me dead, I would already be gone.

Zeus taps his fingertips together and peers over them as though I've broken some line that I didn't know existed. "They are being acclimated to Loge. Not everyone is blessed as you are with an inside ticket to our world. We need to know that we can trust those we've allowed to come here. Jackson vouched for you. Please don't give me a reason to doubt his judgment. Now, is there anything else?"

The question that repeats over and over in my mind swims to the surface. I draw a breath, pushing aside my fear. "Why didn't you respond?" I ask.

"Respond?" Zeus gives me a quizzical look, and then reading my mind, replaces the look with a grin. "Ah, I see not all has been disclosed." His eyes flicker to Jackson, then he stands, addressing the crowd. "Our new resident wants to know why we didn't respond to the attack on our kind."

Everyone erupts in laughter. Everyone except Jackson, who turns to me, pleading. "I was waiting to tell you until we got settled at home. I didn't want to upset you while your body was trying to heal. His plan—the strategy…" I look from person to person behind me, all of them enjoying some hidden joke at my expense. I eye Jackson, and then seeing the obvious, that he has once again kept something from me, I take a deliberate step away from him, anger raging in my chest so intensely I have to grit my teeth together to keep from screaming.

"Now, now," Zeus says, "you cannot blame him. He only just learned."

"Learned what?" I spit out.

Zeus smiles. "Do you know how many deaths we suffered?"

"Obviously not."

"Zero," he says, his smile widening. "And the humans? Well, the numbers reported continue to climb. Our kind has inveigled the humans for centuries. Nothing we do is ever by chance."

Nothing by chance. Those were Emmy's words when I'd first woken in the Panacea and asked about my becoming an Ancient. But it isn't like Zeus knew how many humans were healed over the years. Or did he? My eyes rise to his. *Did you?*

Zeus tilts his head in a calculated way, his mouth set like a relaxed predator, waiting for the kill. "Inveigle: to entice, manipulate, bait."

I lunge forward. "You sick, piece of—"

"Don't." Jackson grabs me.

I glare at him, fighting to free myself from his grasp. "Do you even know what it means to tell the truth? So much for honesty. Let me go. Now."

Zeus tsks. "Testy, testy. We shall see how long it takes to remove the wild within you."

I can't find the will to say anything in return. Because this means everything is orchestrated, everything a lie. Zeus intentionally had the Ancients heal humans, so when the neurotoxin released it would backfire on us, killing our own kind. I may be safe, but what about my family and friends? How will they survive when the enemy is always one step ahead? They won't, unless...

Jackson gives me a knowing look, his face otherwise blank, but in that brief glance, that brief moment, I read his intent. This war has just begun. He doesn't agree with Zeus. He plans to fight. But after everything he's done, how can I trust him? I can't, I won't. For now, I'm on my own.

I wait as Zeus studies me, his head tilted to the side as though he's trying to puncture through my thoughts. "If nothing else, then step forward for the assignation."

I hesitate, sure that if I edge any closer to Zeus I'll attack him and end up dead.

"Not now, Ari," Jackson whispers.

I dip my head and draw a long breath, then step forward. The female healer seated at the furthest right side stands, motioning for me to come to her first. She is younger than Emmy, much younger. Her eyes are sharp and her face is free of wrinkles. Her hair is a deep red that is almost blinding to the eye.

I stand before her, my head higher than I feel, and wait for instruction. She looks at me, and I look back, and for a moment I fear that I've missed something important. Maybe I'm un-assignationable. Then she reaches out her hand to me, and I extend my own. She takes my hand in hers, as Emmy often does, and suddenly I know this must be how they "read" us. All those times Emmy took my hand I had assumed she was just being motherly. Now I know she was checking for herself what

I refused to say—how I was feeling, what I was thinking. Emmy has held my hand every day of the twenty-one days that I have been on Loge, and all the while I felt I was shadowing my true intentions. I underestimated her, and for whatever reason, this makes me appreciate her all the more.

The female healer doesn't speak as she holds my hand. She doesn't introduce herself or smile or even hint that we are in close proximity. Instead, she stares into my eyes and I hers, and then she nods to me. "Thank you," she says, before returning to her seat, and the next healer beside her stands. I move from healer to healer, each holding my hand for all of five minutes before sitting, and when I'm done I return to my place beside Jackson, feeling confused and exposed. What did they see within me? Back home, I would have liked to be a Chemist, like my mom, if I weren't set to become the commander of Engineers, like Dad. But here, I'm not sure. Maybe school work.

The healers each pass a sheet of paper down to Zeus, who reads them in turn, then stacks them and sets the pile in front of him. His eyes find mine and I can tell that he isn't happy with their consensus. "It is a majority decision that you, Ari Alexander, will become an RES upon completion of internal analysis and implantation. Gildan will escort you," he says, pointing to a male Ancient to his left.

I release a shaky breath. RES. Of course I would be an RES. And now I'm going to train to kill humans. An overwhelming feeling of nausea swirls through my stomach, and I have to swallow several times to keep myself from getting sick. My eyes find Zeus and I'm surprised to see he looks as disappointed with this assessment as I am. If he doesn't want me to become an RES, why not just say so? I start to ask him as much, when my thoughts stop on what he just said. "Wait—implantation?" I glance from Zeus to Jackson and back.

The corners of Zeus's mouth curl, and I realize he gets

pleasure out of making people uncomfortable, pushing them mentally. "You are a member of my army now." A haunting laugh floats from his throat, circling around the room, fear on its wake from the other Ancients in the room. "Welcome to Triad."

CHAPTER 3

I lay flat against a cold table, cringing as the healer beside me—the scary one from the Lexis incident earlier—shoves needle after needle into my arm, each one causing me to drift further from reality.

I can't remember how I arrived here. Stairway or elevator, a single door or a passageway, I'm not sure. I remember leaving Zeus and then lying on this table, undressed except for a makeshift cloth covering the important parts of my body. Zeus had dismissed everyone in the room except Jackson and me, his eyes on me while the other Ancients left. Then once the door closed behind the last Ancient, he walked over and shook my hand, as though we were old friends instead of enemies. I expected his skin to be cold, something about his look and attitude demanded cold skin, but nothing like this. It felt dry, the cold biting, like jumping into a stream during the winter. And the look on his face, a dare of some sorts, a checkmate, like he had me in sight and was going to enjoy watching me squirm.

Then without another word, I was escorted away by his guard, Jackson at my side. They must have forced Jackson to leave, because I'm alone in the room except for the guard by the door and the scary healer next to me. She bears the same green dress as before, another long needle in hand. "Calm your mind, child," she says, brushing one of her hands easily over my eyes. For the briefest second, I want to open them back up, but then a thick fog spreads over my brain, seeping down my neck and through my body. Warmth and relaxation move over me. I don't feel or hear anything else after that. No light, no fear, no worry. I feel at peace for the first time since arriving here, and that's when I realize what I must be experiencing—sleep. Peaceful sleep, void of the nightmares that have plagued me for weeks. I let my body succumb to it, grateful for the moment of serenity.

But then I wake.

Chaos reigns inside my brain in overload. Intense feelings—fear, worry, happiness, love—then words, jarring me from my rest and into the unknown. I feel the hardness of the table on my back, yet everything is spinning. I reach out for something to help steady me and feel a warm hand wrap around mine.

"It's okay," Jackson says close to my ear. "It calms down. Just breathe." And it's too much. I feel him, Jackson, his every single thought toward me. He's worried. No, he's sad. Afraid. Worried. Sad—I can't process it. I can't think. His feelings mingle with my own, one orange, the other yellow, shades of the rainbow, one beside the other, never mixing, yet so close it's difficult to see where one ends and the other begins. Then a third slips into the color spectrum and I want to throw up—I'm going to throw up. Red. Hate. So much hate. There is no other word to describe it. A tear traces down my face, the sudden change in emotion so overwhelming if I could speak I would beg for relief.

Jackson wipes away the tear. "Breathe. Just breathe."

I suck in a jagged breath, while tears continue to run down my face, pooling under my neck, wetting my hair. *I want the red to leave. Please make it leave.*

"Leave now," Jackson commands, the color coming off him changing from orange to black.

"You are in my building, lest you forget," Zeus says, and I feel him near, but not just his presence. His emotions, his thoughts, all of them directed at me. I open my eyes to see him leaning over me, a smile on his face, while waves of hate continue to lap through me, suffocating my mind and senses. "Pain is an object of the mind, like feelings. You were taught to ignore pain, yes?"

I don't respond, though of course he's right. Dad taught me at a young age to release pain from my body, especially when exposed to it for long periods of time. He used to place weights in my arms and make me hold them out to my side, like a *T*, until my arms shook from the burning. If I admitted to the pain, I had to hold them for thirty minutes longer. If the weights dropped from my grasp, the time doubled the next day.

I focus on Zeus.

"You do the same with this. Learn to shut it out, commanding it to the surface when you want it to work, silencing it when you don't. Otherwise, you will become a statistical void and will be handled. Superior minds are my specialty. The mind is beautiful and complex. It must be shaped into form like a muscle." His gaze rests on mine, the hate now doubling, swarming through me, threatening to pull me under. "Have no doubt, *Commander Alexander*, I will shape you, too."

Jackson straightens, anger coiling from him into me. "That's enough."

Zeus smiles. "Very well."

I close my eyes as he leaves, allowing the hate to dissipate from my mind before I reopen them. "I have the implant now, don't I? The one that detects feelings and stress."

Jackson's eyes turn cold, never leaving the door where Zeus just left. "Yes. You're officially an RES now."

• • •

An hour later, Jackson helps me find my clothes and after I'm dressed, we leave, him telling me we're going home. Thankfully, there is no one on the streets outside. I'm not sure I could walk if a bunch of Ancient emotions hit me all at once. Jackson's are enough, though I find he's shadowing some of them from me, controlling them in my presence—or maybe in everyone's presence.

We head down the main central road, brief flutters of emotions hitting me as we walk. I'm guessing the closer someone is the stronger the sensation. Here, with no one in sight, I feel curiosity hit me—light blue. Happiness—pink. And an emotion I can't put my finger on, though the shade is a deep gray. Something so ugly can't be pleasant.

"Are you okay?" Jackson asks.

I shrug, unsure of what exactly I am. "It's just…different."

"Triad or your new gift?"

I almost laugh at the word "gift." Is that what they call it here? As though it's a privilege to know the feelings of everyone around me. I think it's a punishment, and it isn't lost on me that Zeus wanted me equipped the moment I was healthy enough to sustain it. There has to be a reason for that, too. I glance sideways at Jackson, realizing he's waiting for me to answer.

"Everything," I say and stare out over the bridge as we cross over it. Everything is odd here. The materials similar, yet different. The bridge is some combination of stone and wood, hard and smooth like stone, but with long lines of texture that remind me of wood. I don't know what it really is and I'm not in the mood to ask.

"When did you find out that Zeus manipulated the strategy against us?"

Jackson looks directly at me. "Right before I came to get you. I wanted to tell you immediately, I did, but not there, where everyone was listening. You'll learn here that almost everyone reports to Zeus. It isn't safe to talk openly about things like that. I would have told you the moment we got home. I should have known you would ask."

I nod. I can tell from the bright white that slips into my mindthat he's telling the truth. "So what do we do?"

He shakes his head and lowers his voice. "Not here."

The bridge ends at a road that's again a new material, this one black with specks of silver in it, that curves around a large building into the first section of homes. We cross over into a neighborhood, all small white homes with yellow roofs. Each home has a front porch with benches on it like everyone sits outside and chats at night. I'm preparing to ask my first question, when Jackson stops at the third house in, left-hand side.

"This is us," he says, and then, sensing my unease, adds, "It's going to be fine. They're probably not even home right now."

"How many are there?" I check from house to house, curious if there is anyone outside, watching us arrive, but the streets are empty. "And aren't you a little young to be living by yourselves?"

"We section off from our parents at sixteen here. And there are two of us living here, three including you."

Jackson hesitates for a second, and I turn to look up at him, curious to know why he suddenly seems more nervous than I do. Maybe he's worried his roommate won't like me. Finally, he releases a long breath and motions to the front door, which is a sight of its own right. The door is made of a stained wood, but that isn't the unusual part. Carved into the wood is a giant face, its expression that of judgment—arched eyebrows, a mouth set into a scowl.

I point to the door as we pass through it. "That's…different."
Jackson laughs. "That's nothing."

I step through the door and realize immediately what he means. We are in a large common room with wooden walls etched from floor to ceiling with pictorial indentations that seem to tell a story I've never heard before. Ancients facing the sun, rays darting out from their hands. Ancients kneeled with their palms flat against the ground. An etching of the Earth with a single word above it: *Salvation*.

"They're Vill's work," Jackson says. "He's worked on every wall in the house."

"Vill?"

"Yeah, my roommate. Here, I'll show you around." He reaches for my hand, then drops his back down, causing an uneasiness to settle between us. Jackson points at the hallway, and I follow him out of the room.

The hallway is fairly short, with two doors on either side. And like the main room, Vill's marked this area too, though here he's painted every inch with tiny images that combine to make a larger picture. It's the sort of thing you could stare at for hours and still not see everything or understand its meaning.

"The last one on the right is Vill," Jackson says, pointing to a deep brown door. "And this is ours." He opens the last door on the left to a room brimming with light. A giant window takes up much of the back wall, and positioned in front of it is a bed twice as large as mine at the Panacea. Instead of cream blankets and linens, Jackson's are all a deep olive, manly against the almost black wooden bed frame. A hand carved shelf occupies the right wall (no doubt Vill's handiwork), while the left stands bare except for a beaded curtain, that I imagine leads to a closet. I turn to the wall closest to me, my eyes widening. It's a painting, the image portrayed so perfectly it looks real. The background is the forest that borders Sydia, but it's not dark or scary, it's full of light, life, almost like it belongs here instead of there. If not for the cityscape in the distance, I wouldn't be sure. I allow my eyes to absorb every inch of it, feeling so homesick in that moment it's all I can do not to cry. But then my eyes settle on a small figure in the center of the painting, the detail so impeccable I'm sure of what it is—who it is—even before I have to ask.

"Is that…?"

Jackson leans against the door and musses his hair with both hands, before glancing up at the painting. "It's you."

"When was this done? And how? Vill's never met me." I'm not fighting in the painting, or shooting a gun, or doing any one of the many things that define me. Instead, I'm seated on the ground in a bed of leaves, staring up into the open sky, the trees surrounding me like old friends. I look happy, peaceful, not at all the way I see myself.

"A year ago, I guess. He pulled from my memory. He wasn't satisfied with my descriptions, so he just…"

I turn to look at him, my heart swelling though I try to push it away. A year ago. That was before I found out he was an Ancient, before we had become…whatever we were. I don't know what to say.

Jackson lowers his head, scratching his chin uncomfortably, but I can't take my eyes off him. He glances up sideways, his hair once again shadowing his eyes. "What can I say? For me, it has always been you." He breaks the connection before I can respond and motions toward the bed. "You can sleep here. I'll have the floor. If it's okay we're in the same room? If you want more space, then I can crash with Vill. Just let me know."

I shake my head. "No, it's fine. I don't want you to leave your room." I want to tell him he can sleep in the bed too, but I'm not ready for that. I need to get to know him—the real him—separate from all the conspiracy and lies. I have more questions that I can possibly handle, each thing bringing on a slew of new ones.

Jackson tucks his hands into his pockets and nods toward me. "Ask. I know you have questions. I'll tell you whatever you want to know."

I think it through and settle on what I want to know the most. "How is everyone?" I don't elaborate—he knows who I mean. He has tried to talk to them several times since I've been here, each time giving me updates, though I've noticed they're becoming more and more vague.

"The same. Different, but yet the same." His head bobs once, like the description couldn't be more perfect. "Your dad is still commander, your mom still a Chemist. Gretchen is still Gretchen. Yet, they're all different, changed, aged. I don't know. I think they're putting on a show for everyone, but inside they're all someone else now. I think they're planning something. I don't know what. And Law, he's…harder, or maybe he just hates me."

The memory of Law's face when he told me he and Jackson were brothers slips into my mind. Even after all this time, it's hard to process. I want to know more about Jackson's father, how he became involved with President Cartier, Lawrence's mother. If it happened while she was with Law's father—who died years ago now—or if it was before since Jackson is older than Law. I don't know.

Jackson looks away, and I know he must have heard what I was thinking. I walk over to the shelf Vill built and start examining one of a dozen of the mini sculptures situated there. They are all different. Some are flowers, others strange creatures I've never seen before. With each painting or sculpture, Vill's sanity becomes more and more questionable. I glance up at Jackson to see him smirking at me. "Ah, he's not so bad. Just…expressive."

"So you say." I switch to something less personal. "When can I talk to my mom? Or my dad? Does he still seem on edge?"

Jackson swallows. "Yes. I can't tell if it has to do with him knowing who I am now or if there's something deeper going on. I think it's the latter. Something may have changed there and for whatever reason they can't or aren't willing to tell me about it. Maybe once they know you're okay…We'll see. Your mom will be happy to see you. She'll be there tonight."

My eyes dart up from the tiny tree figurine in my hand. "My mom. What has she said? Does she sound okay? Wait, did you say tonight?" I repeat, unable to keep the excitement from my voice. I love all my family and friends, all of them, but I miss my mom the most. I miss knowing someone was around who supported me no matter what, who thought I could do anything. I miss the straight love I felt when I was with her. I miss smelling her simple, clean perfume long after she released me from a hug. "Can I talk to her now?"

Jackson's face softens. "We have our first meeting tonight."

"Tonight?"

"Tonight."

I smile. Tonight, I get to talk to my family.

CHAPTER 4

"Hey, there's food," a voice calls from down the hall.

Jackson and I step into the main room and the smell of cooked food wafts through the air. "We eat outside. Is that okay?"

I nod and we head outside. It's dark now, the sky peaceful. Three chairs sit in haphazard order around the front porch, one already full. The boy looks younger than I imagined. He has black hair and olive skin and a look about him that suggests he's always thinking.

"You must be Vill," I say, walking over to greet him.

"Indeed. And I know who you are." He looks at me as though he knows much more about me than just my name or my face. "It's nice to meet you, Ari."

Jackson pulls up the other two chairs and hands me a plate of food. It's full of some cooked greens that look like grass, more bocas, and something else that might be meat—or it could be charred bread. And while the food is different, it's still food, which again seems odd. I'm not sure what I expected them to eat. Honestly, I'd never given much thought to what they ate.

"It's real food, if that's what you're wondering," Jackson says, answering my unasked question.

"So what is it?"

"Our diets consist of the vital nutrients necessarily to sustain our bodies. Nothing more. Nourishment over taste, if you will," Vill says, and I realize that for whatever reason I like him already. He has something pure about him, like he'd never think anything but the most genuine thoughts. It's refreshing.

Jackson goes back in to grab us drinks, and as soon as he's gone, Vill leans in close to me. "How are you holding up?"

Good. Horribly. Both answers seem appropriate. I settle on, "I'm okay."

Vill nods. "The transition can be unsettling."

Unsettled is the perfect way to describe me, and again, I get the feeling Vill understands me on a deeper level than our solo introduction would suggest. "I like your work," I say, hoping to change the subject. He looks away, and I sense that he doesn't like attention.

"My mind operates on a continous cycle. It helps me focus."

"Yeah, I know what you mean." I think of my trainings back home with Dad. He required me to train with him personally each morning at six a.m. At first, I worried over what he thought, how I was doing, would I make him proud. But eventually, I learned that if I dropped all thought and let my body take over, that my mind became more focused on the task at hand. Doing something, activating my muscles, helped me in that way. I guess Vill is the same, though our outlets are different.

Jackson comes back with our drinks and takes a sip of his. A single drop remains on his lip and he licks it away. A warmth moves over me, my mind replaying our first kiss, the way his fingertips gently slipped down my face as though I was too delicate to touch with anything but a light hand. I can almost feel them on me now.

I jump up, shaken by the memory, and realizing my error, glance over at Jackson. His eyes burn into mine. He knows what

I was thinking, felt my reaction to the memory. I have to control my thoughts around him, now more than ever. I don't know if I can ever truly trust Jackson again and I won't allow myself to get involved with someone I don't trust. Besides, I have more pressing matters at hand, like Cybil, like finding the humans.

Still…the kiss hits in my mind again, this time followed by a sharp stab in my chest. I squeeze my eyes shut and reopen them, pushing the memory as far from reach as possible.

"Are you all right?" Vill asks.

I glance up, embarassed that I've allowed my mind to drift so far from reality. "Uh, yeah. Yes, I'm fine. I could use a shower. Do you have showers here?"

"Of course," he says.

"Can I take one?"

Jackson sets down his plate. "Sure. After."

"After what?"

His eyes balance on mine. "The call. Our meeting is in less than five minutes."

Suddenly, everything inside me is awake and alert.

I follow Jackson back inside and into the kitchen, though all I can see is two stone pits and a silver square that I suppose is a refrigerator. Behind and to the far left of the pits lies a door with thick bolts at the top and bottom, securing it shut. Jackson unbolts it to reveal a set of stone stairs that descend into pitch-blackness. He nods for me to go ahead of him. As soon as the door closes, a light pops on above us, and then Jackson starts down the stairs. We round the corner at the bottom and into a room so alive with technology it makes Dad's office back home look archaic. Three large screens hang on the back wall, the desk below them full of various tiny figurines, some complete, others unfinished. To the right and left of the screens are various silver boxes, each with green and red lights that take turns flickering on and off. It's the most advanced room I've witnessed since coming here.

"What is this place?" I whisper.

"My office, you could say. It's where I do research and where I communicate with Earth. No one knows it's here other than Vill. He practically lives down here, as I'm sure you can tell," he says, pointing at the figurines. "He actually helped me build it. He's brilliant. Really brilliant. He's also the one who figured out how to tap into Earth's intergalactic satellite frequency. That's how we can talk to them."

I take a seat in one of the chairs in front of the main screen. "But how can you send a message to the satellite without Zeus seeing it?"

Jackson smiles. "That's all Vill. Years ago, Zeus sent a satellite into orbit to create a wormhole that would allow superluminal communication with Earth. Earth did the same, so once both were activated, we had a way of sending a message, using our satellilte, to the wormhole, which then propelled the message directly to Earth's satellite. As you can imagine, we continued to work on the technology and created a more advanced satellite and a new wormhole a year ago when Zeus began questioning Earth's leaders' willingness to coexist. That original satellite was still in orbit, unused, so Vill hacked into it. Zeus will eventually find out, but for now, we have a means of communicating with Earth that is virtually undetectable."

So Vill is more than an artist, he's also something of a genius. "How does the satellite create a wormhole?"

Jackson pushes his chair away from the desk. "It uses dark matter to send rotating lasers to a specific place in space. The lasers stir up space until the energy changes and a wormhole is created. The wormhole then allows us to communcate at faster than light speeds. Superluminal communication."

Jackson flips on the screens, which resemble a T-screen back home but more advanced—much more advanced. The main screen seems to detect what he wants from it without him having to do anything at all.

"It's like it senses you or something," I say, edging closer to the screen.

"We tapped into RES transmitter technology so the communicator is sensitive enough to pull from our thought waves. See everything, including thoughts, produces an energy that once released into the reality around us, changes the energy of our surroundings. So, if you're able to harness it, then virtually anything becomes possible. It's metaphysics."

I shake my head. "I'm lost. But it sounds amazing."

"It is. I'll teach you, in time. Or Vill can. He gets it on a much deeper level than I do. I tend to rely on my strength, where as Vill leans completely on his mind. He believes the mind can overpower strength."

"And you don't agree?"

"I think we need both, but I have a hard time buying the mind over matter thing, at least as a fighter. We need our minds, sure, but strength closes a fight. Anyway." He points at the screen. "There's a small delay, but we should be receiving the feed any moment."

The screen is black except for a tiny yellow dot that flickers in the center. After a while I assume nothing is going to happen, then the screen shifts and I'm staring at a long table full of people in business attire or all black Engineer clothing. I glance from one to the other, taking them all in, when my eyes find the far left side of the table and it's all I can do not to hug the screen. Seated at the end is my dad, dressed in his usual Engineer attire. His commander pin glints in the light. He smiles a bit when he sees me, then washes it away and threads his fingers together on the table, all business. My mom is beside him, wearing her Chemist lab coat, and unlike my dad, she doesn't try to surpress her joy. A hand goes to her mouth and I can see tears in her eyes. She smiles and I smile back.

I don't want to look away from them, but I can tell this is a formal gathering of important people, and the Operative in me rises to the surface. I take a seat beside Jackson and eye the rest of the group. There is one empty chair on the opposite side and left from my dad. Jackson notices the chair as well and nods toward it, but before either of us can ask if we should wait on the person to arrive, a door behind the table opens and Lawrence enters the room, only he no longer looks like the Lawrence I remember.

His easiness has been replaced by a rigidity that is so foreign on him I have to look twice to be sure it's really him. His hair is cut short and gelled, and he's wearing the standard Parliament suit—crisp white shirt, black coat and slacks, red tie. He doesn't look at me as he takes his seat, and suddenly I'm aware of the mood in the room. Everyone is tense. Some nervously glancing around. Others tapping their fingers together. It's as though this conversation holds tremendous importance and must be handled with care.

Lawrence nods to an older, balding man beside him, seated across from my dad at the right end of the table. The man is dressed exactly like Lawrence and half the other people at the table. He stares forward, glancing from Jackson to me. "Thank you for joining us."

Jackson sits back in his chair. "Of course, though we didn't realize this was a formal meeting."

I'm impressed with Jackson's forwardness, though the look on the gentleman's face says he doesn't share my opinion.

"I am Kelvin Lancaster, Lead Chemist and acting President of the United States."

"Wait, President?" I say. "Law, what happened to—?"

Kelvin interrupts. "All will be explained in time, but for now, we have important matters to discuss."

Jackson tenses beside me and I know he's thinking what I'm thinking. Who does this guy think he is? I eye Dad to find him staring at me, a hard look on his face. His head twitches almost imperceptably. He's telling me to wait. I straighten in my chair, forcing patience. "Very well."

Kelvin nods. "Thank you. As Mr. Castello has informed you, I'm sure, we are communicating through a satellite frequency that taps into an unused satellite orbiting Loge. The frequencey is secure, for now, though we have no way of knowing how long that security will remain. For that reason, it's important that we discuss all important matters and actions immediately."

I glance briefly to my parents, and then say without pause, "Mr. Lancaster, we appreciate the urgency of the situation, but I have to ask why you expect us to assist in whatever plan you're about to offer? Your people created execution bases for all infected humans, sentencing them to death, including myself. Why would I trust you now?"

Dad sits up to answer, but Kelvin raises a hand to stop him. "Your point is valid, Ms. Alexander, but please understand that we witnessed one of the fastest epidemics in human history. We had no way of knowing why people were becoming infected and felt it necessary to quickly act to protect humankind. It was a tough decision. As all decisions such as this are hard. But we now know our error and have acted accordingly."

"Meaning you are no longer killing the infected?"

Kelvin motions toward my mother, who speaks. "Ari, we have treated all who remained on Earth, and are happy to report that we have suffered no more casulaties. It took three experimental healing serums to develop the cure, but we found one, and all execution bases were destroyed. I think we agree that those early measures were rash, if not horrendous."

Whispers of assent sound around the room. "We will not be making the same mistake twice. We want to get our people home."

"And that brings us to you." Kelvin leans forward, his eyes squarely on me. "We have reason to believe that Zeus Castello plans to attack Earth in two weeks time. We would like to prevent this from happening, while simultaneously bringing all humans back to Earth."

Jackson sits up. "And what about the Ancients who want nothing more than a peaceful life? What are your plans for them?"

"We are prepared to allow them to come to Earth permanently," Kelvin answers.

"If…?" Jackson asks.

Kelvin returns his gaze to me, and Law speaks up for the first time. "Ari, we have devised a plan that we believe will work, but for that plan to be successful, we need to remove our greatest threat."

"Which is?"

Mom looks down, and Dad shakes his head, both clearly upset.

"What is it?" I ask, glancing from them back to Law. "What are you asking me to do?"

"You won't be alone," Law says. "We have two Operatives on Loge to help you, both undercover." I picture Cybil, wrapped in cloths. She must be one of their spies, but how can she be of help if she's all but comatose? "It's dangerous, we know that, but we can't think of another option. It's either this or —"

"Just tell me."

Everyone's eyes land on me, but it's Kelvin who speaks. "We need you to kill Zeus Castello."

CHAPTER 5

We sit in silence for a long time, staring at the now black screen. They want me to kill Zeus. *Zeus!* I run my hands over my face. "What do you think?" I ask.

Jackson stands and starts sorting through a stack of paper on the table beside him, his look distant. "I don't know what to think. Honestly, I'm surprised they mentioned it in front of me."

"Yeah, that surprised me, too, though what choice did they have?"

"True."

"What do you think of what they're asking?"

He draws a long breath. "I think it's a death sentence."

"I thought you may say that."

He turns around, his eyes on mine. "But if you have to do it, surprise is our best defense. He'll ask to see you tomorrow. I'll give you a gun." Jackson starts for the stairs. "I'll make sure I'm closeby just to be safe. It could work. He might be expecting something, but he would never expect you to try something so soon."

"Wait. Tomorrow? You can't be serious. We should plan this out. Think it through. Tomorrow is too—"

Jackson laughs, the sound so cold it sends a shiver down my back. "Is there really a good time to try to kill someone like Zeus? The best chance we have is to catch him off guard. He's arrogant. He'll believe that you are too afraid and vulnerable right now to try anything."

I swallow, letting his words and the logic in them sink in. He's right. I take my hair out of the elastic I had used to pull it up, and then pile it on top of my head and wrap the elastic around it again, my mind focused on what I have to do. I need to think.

"I need a shower."

"Come on, I'll show you."

I follow Jackson back into the house. A shower is exactly what I need to clear my head so I can think through how to make this happen. We walk down the hallway to a door at the end of the hall I hadn't noticed before. He pushes through and we step out into what can only be described as paradise. Absolute paradise.

The backyard is small, tiny even, but it's fenced in by walls of large flowers, all different colors. Situated in the back center of the yard is a circular, stone something, about the size of a closet, with an open top and a metallic showerhead hanging from one end to the center.

I hesitate. "That's the shower? Outside? What about the bathroom in general?"

He grins, though the smile doesn't reach his eyes. "Don't worry. That part is inside, along with a cleansing drum, which is what most use. I had them add this shower out here after I'd spent so much time on Earth. Somehow I no longer feel clean unless I'm bathing in water."

"So, I'm guessing a cleansing drum doesn't use water? What does it use?"

His grin widens. "Nothing crazy. I'll show you tomorrow. For now, this has everything you need. Step inside and the water will turn on automatically. There are towels in the bin beside it. Take your time."

I wait for Jackson to go back inside. I don't want him to see how uneasy I feel. Once I'm sure he's gone, I reach for the small latch that keeps the shower door closed. I unhook it and step inside. The floor of the shower is the same stone as the walls. One wall is lined with shelves containing liquids and solids that I can only imagine must be soap and shampoo and other toiletries. A second passes, then the water turns on, sending a warm shower over me—and my clothes, which I wasn't willing to take off in the open.

I slip out of my clothes and embrace the water, standing there for several seconds with my eyes closed, letting it soak me through and through. Wash away the aches of my mind and heart. It feels good, almost freeing. With my eyes still closed, I let my mind focus on Zeus. I think through everything I know about him, which isn't much. It would be better if I were planning to kill someone I knew more about. His daily activities. His strength and weaknesses. Zeus appears to be elderly, but something about the way his eyes never leave you makes me think he's more agile than he looks.

I stay in the shower much longer than is appropriate, and I wonder if there are rules about things like this. Time constraints or something. But no alarms sound, and no one comes knocking on the door. So I stay as long as I can handle it, until my fingers and toes wrinkle from the overexposure. Then I drape a towel around me and move back inside, glad the halls are clear, and slip into Jackson's empty room.

I take my time combing my fingers through my hair, then search the room for some clothes. Behind the beaded curtain is a small closet with one rack of clothes and lots of tiny drawers built into the walls. Inside the right-hand side drawers are clothes, all my size. I can't differentiate the pajamas from the everyday clothes, so I just pull out something that seems comfortable enough and slip it on.

I sit down on the bed, my legs crossed, and wait for Jackson to come back. I wouldn't say I feel ready for what I have to do tomorrow, but I've prepared my mind that I have no choice. Now, I need to see the gun he wants me to use. Feel it in my hand. Practice pulling it from where ever I plan to stow it.

I hear a knock outside the door, then Jackson's voice. "Dressed?"

"Yes," I call.

He slips into the room and sits in a chair beside his closet. His eyes sweep over my face, my wet hair, down my body, then back. He swallows hard.

"Okay."

"Okay, what?" he asks.

"I'm ready. Where's the gun? I need to practice."

Jackson watches me for a moment. "Ari, maybe I should—"

"No. It has to be me."

He sighs heavily before going to his closet and opening the third drawer from the top. He sets the clothes all on the floor, pops out the wooden base, and reaches in and grabs two guns, placing each on the bed beside me. "One of these should work."

I pick up the one on my left. It's small, about the size of my hand, polished silver and black exterior. I lift it up, close one eye, and peek through the sight at one of Vill's figurine's on Jackson's shelf. "Are all those drawers loaded down like that one?" I grin up at him. "If I didn't know any better, I would say you were a spy among spies."

He doesn't return the smile. "This is serious."

"I know." I return my attention to the gun, letting it balance in my hands. Pointing it at various things around the room. I wish I could shoot it. Only then would I really know, but there is no way I could fire a gun at this hour without drawing some attention. "Does it have a laser?" I ask, not seeing one affixed to the weapon, but it could be built it, like a trick knife that can do numerous things.

"No. Most of our guns have lasers, so the screening at Zeus's office will be set to detect the laser. This one should get you through without a problem."

"And what about the sound? Lasers are quieter than bullets."

He reaches back into the drawer, pulls out a tiny cylinder, and screws it onto the tip of the gun. "Not when you have a silencer."

I point the gun at a small tiger on Jackson's shelf and fire. "True."

Jackson laughs, the sound producing such a change in the air that I stop to look at him, mezmerized by his smile. "Vill's going to kill you," he says. "That was a favorite."

"Yeah, well, he has thousands around here. He'll live." I place the gun down gently on the bed and pick up the other. It's heavier than the first, feeling almost twice as heavy in my hands. I let it balance, eyeing another one of Vill's creations, but I don't shoot. I can tell it's not the right fit. "I'll go with the first."

"Okay." The playful expression from before disappears from his face, and he returns the unwanted gun to the third drawer. He sits down in front of me, his demeanor serious, controlled, like he was back in the Panacea. Was that only today? It feels like weeks ago now.

"This is what you're going to do," he says. "You'll go see Zeus as he's requested. Act natural. He'll want to see you in his office with no one else around, though of course he has surveillance watching. He likes to face his windows while he talks, leaving you behind him so you can't see his face. Ask him how he came to control Triad. It's a lengthy story that he loves to tell. When he gets to the part about building the Healer's

Wall, he'll go to his windows to look out over Triad, to look at his creation. That's when you shoot."

I crack one of my knuckles, planning to stop at just the one, but before I know it, I've cracked all the joints in my left hand. "How do you know he'll tell the story? He might say it's none of my business or something."

"Oh, he'll tell it. Zeus's ego is too large for him to *not* tell it. Just remember to wait until he gets to the part about the wall. I've seen him tell this story a thousand times and he always goes to his windows when he gets to that part."

"Okay." I reach behind me and slid the gun under one of the pillows. "For good luck."

"Ari, you don't have to do this. We can tell them no. We can figure out a different way."

I fumble with the hem of my shirt, pulling a loose thread until it unravels much of the hem. "No. They're right. There is no other way. As long as Zeus lives, we're all in danger."

Jackson starts to argue, but seeing the resolve on my face, goes for the lights instead. "Well, get some sleep. You'll need it."

I slip under the covers and instantly smell Jackson on the sheets. They smell earthy and clean and I find myself burying deeper into one of the pillows, comforted by the smell. Jackson turns out the light, and keeping to his word, slips down onto a makeshift bed on the floor. After that, silence finds us and soon the ringing in my ears is replaced by Jackson's smooth breathing. I lean over the side of the bed and watch him sleep. His right arm is drapped lazily over his head against the pillow, his hair scattered in a mess, shading his closed eyes. His chest rises and falls in easy rhythm, and for a moment, I forget who he is and what he's done and remember that aside from all that, he's only a boy…and I've just agreed to kill his grandfather.

I lay back down and close my eyes, allowing my thoughts to drift in and out of focus. Before long I'm asleep, my thoughts replaced with a nightmare—the same nightmare I've had since arriving here. I'm back at the site of the execution base where President Cartier had ordered all infected humans be brought to be killed. Jackson comes for me. And then I watch from a distance as a bomb drops over the site, killing everyone in one devastating blow. But this time, someone enters the dream. Red fills my mind, growing so dark it's almost black, and while I can't see him, I know it's Zeus. The bomb drops, as it always does, but instead of me waking, a chilling laugh echoes all around me, growing louder and louder until I'm left with nothing but the screams of the innocent...and the laugh of the wicked.

• • •

Sirens startle me awake, pulling me from the nightmare. I cover my ears with my hands, and Jackson leaps from the floor and goes to the door, listening, then jerks it open. "You stay here, understand?"

I shake my head. "No. I'm coming."

"Stay here."

"No." I'm up and to him before he can argue and I know I'll hear about this later. I'm not the sort of person to wait to hear what might be happening. I want to see it. And when we reach the front porch, I see I'm not alone. Everyone is outside, most disoriented. Vill walks up beside me. I look around for Jackson. He's already down the street, edging toward the source of the sound.

"What's happening?" I ask Vill.

"Someone's breached the border." He points to the Healer's Wall that surrounds Triad, where a flying craft has someone pinpointed below a strobe light. I can't tell what's happening or hear anything beyond the siren. We all stand on our porches or the street, frozen, watching as the light grows closer and closer to the man. And then just like that, the man is sucked into the craft and the light disappears.

I stumble back, my hands to my mouth. "What did they just do?"

"Back inside," Jackson says, rushing toward us. "Now."

I hear the sound of footsteps coming down the main street and see armed men and women marching, others continuing to the other streets. This is nothing like what Jackson had said about Loge, all peaceful beings who wanted happiness for everyone. This is madness and terror.

The Ancients on the streets all head back into their homes like us. Jackson closes the door behind Vill and me but remains on the porch. I edge over to a nearby window and peer out as one of the armed guards walks up our steps to Jackson. They exchange words I can't make out, then the guard continues on down the street.

"What was that about?" I ask, as Jackson comes through the door.

He glances behind him as though the guards can hear him through the door. "One of the infected humans escaped."

"Escaped? I didn't realize they were being held captive. What aren't you telling me?"

Jackson rubs his eyes and sits on the table in the common room. It's another one of Vill's creations, the legs shaped like folded wings, the face of the table a girl weeping. "The humans are growing restless. There have been some uprisings. Zeus is planning to give them all injections if it doesn't get better. I'm hoping we can stop him first." He gives me a knowing look.

"What sort of injection?"

Vill sits down on one of the chairs. "It's a control substance, allows certain responses to go into hybernation and others to rise to the surface. Basically, it makes it easier to control the person."

"And they're going to give all the humans the injection?"

Vill glances at me, and I realize Jackson has told him the plan. "Unless we stop him first."

Jackson runs a hand through his hair. "I'm gonna shower and head over to see Zeus, now. Be ready in an hour. Your first day as an RES begins today. Remember the plan."

• • •

Jackson arrives back at our house an hour later, his look lethal. He motions for me to follow him without a word, and once outside releases a long exasperated sigh. "Well that was a complete waste of time."

We make our way back to Gaia Road, the main street of Triad, and turn left past the rest of the homes and up toward the Vortex. It's a cool day with a light breeze, the open air comforting after being inside all night. I glance over to where the hovercraft had taken the man just hours before. "What did he say?"

"He said lessons are meant to be learned and refused to talk to me about it any further. Then, as I guessed, he requested that you see him after RES training today."

"So this is it?"

"This is it. Do you have it?"

I turn my ankle and feel the gun press against my leg, just inside my boot. "I have it."

"Good."

A nervousness settles in my stomach, and I walk the rest of the way to the Vortex in silence, listening as Jackson explains the surroundings of Triad. The Healer's Wall that wraps around the city, built so the healers could focus in on specific regions to terraform. Beyond the wall, there is nothing but a dying land until you reach one of the other civilizations on Loge. There are only twelve now, each sanctioned with a trade. Hovercrafts go between regions, bringing food or clothes or whatever, so each civilization can operate soundly. Jackson goes with Zeus monthly to each of the regions, but beyond him, no other Ancients are allowed to leave their designated region.

"Why aren't they allowed to leave?" I ask, stopping him at a second bridge that leads over the Cutana River we sailed down yesterday.

Jackson considers the question for a long moment. "Because Zeus says so."

I glance down at the river, its water full to the banks edge that surround it. Jackson said their water supply was dwindling, but the river shows no signs of a drought. "Is this the only body of water you have? I mean, I know you said your water supply was the issue, but the river looks…" I point down at it.

"It's the healers. They keep Triad alive, the river full. They're the reason we're still alive, but there are very few of them and one hasn't been born in a very long time. There aren't enough of them to sustain us forever, which is why we have to get back to Earth."

We reach the Vortex, just as the two main doors in the center of the building begin to open. Chants and stomping echo from inside, one then the other, the sound a harmony of structure. A series of men and women, all dressed in deep green, all with weapons in hand, march from within the building. There are five rows of Ancients, ten in each line, all of them marching in perfect sequence. They continue out of the building and into the grass just across from it. I realize I've stopped and that I'm staring, but I can't pull my eyes away.

"So that's the RESs?" I ask, awe in my voice. They look so deadly.

"Some of them. Yes."

"Do you have military beyond the RESs? Are there some that aren't spies?"

Jackson pauses. "No. We're fully trained."

"By fully trained, you mean—"

He focuses on me, his voice hard. "We're trained to kill, Ari. And right now the RESs are being trained against one enemy—humans."

I feel my back tighten, anger bubbling to the surface. "And what about the humans who are here? What are they to your RESs?"

Jackson starts for the doors. "Bait."

I freeze, my mouth gaping open. *Bait?* Suddenly, the fear over what I have to do is replaced by a renewed urgency. I have to kill Zeus.

We go through the large main doors of the Vortex, and into an open area so blindingly white that it reminds me of the Chemist labs back home. It's the shape of an octagon, with a door centered within each of the eight walls. I expect Jackson to lead to one of the doors, when instead he turns on me, leans in close to my ear, and whispers, "You're going to have to fight your inner instinct. Remember, you are an RES now. Act like it. If Zeus suspects that you are a threat, he'll kill you without hesitation. And I can't..." He trails off, a pained look on his face. "Just promise me you'll try. Be careful."

I pull away so I can see him clearly. "I will. I promise. But what about you? Aren't you going to be training, too?"

Jackson stands tall as a pair of Ancients enters through the main doors, their eyes on us. "No. I'm the instructor."

I lower my voice. "You mean, you're teaching me? You're my teacher?" This has to be a joke. More Ancients enter, their expressions full of curiosity. I focus on Jackson so I won't worry about what they're thinking.

Jackson bites back a smile. "I'm not your teacher, Alexander. Beginning today, I'm your boss."

"My boss?"

An Ancient walks over dressed in a dark brown T-shirt and pants, his build and demeanor projecting that of someone in a leadership role. "J.C. is there a problem?" he asks, his eyes on me.

"No problem. I will be there in a moment. Alexander here is a new assignee."

The man nods slowly. "All right. Well see you inside." He turns for a set of double doors behind him, but glances back twice at us before disappearing through the doors. I close my eyes and draw a breath. This is going to be painful.

"Okay, *J.C.* where do I go?"

He crosses his arms and smiles. "Through those doors. You'll see the others getting set up."

I give him one more fleeting look before slipping through the double doors. The room is nothing like the entryway to the Vortex. Where it was all bright and shiny and clean, like a lab back home, this room is rugged, the walls wooden, the ceiling high. There are windows cut into the ceiling, letting in the only light in the room outside of a few wall lamps affixed on each of the walls. Situated in the center of the room are rows and rows of pillows, most already full of boys and girls, all appearing to be around my age. The floor, outside of the pillowed seats, is a basic concrete, and glancing around, my first thought is that this room is unforgiving in every way. It's meant to teach you to stay on your feet. Hit a wall or the floor, and you're sure to leave the room covered in bruises or blood. There is no learning by practice here. You learn quickly or your body suffers the consequence of your delay.

I sit on the last pillow closest to the back wall, my legs crossed. No one speaks, most either staring forward with their eyes trained on the opposite wall or their eyes closed, their mouths moving in some silent prayer.

A door on the opposite wall opens and Jackson enters, followed by two Ancients who are twice as big as him and at least six inches taller. They flank him on his right and left side, locking their hands in front of them.

Jackson doesn't smile at the group or hint at any form of kindness. He has a calmness to him that is unsettling, the quiet just before a storm. "You are here because some sliver of existence within you says that you are a born fighter. That you will put your life before others, and stand when others fall. Whether this analysis is correct is yet to be seen, but over the next two weeks we will push you in ways you have never imagined. We will wear down your body. We will challenge your mind. And when we're done, and you're begging for relief, we will push you still more. Only then, when you are at your weakest, will we know if you are truly meant to be an RES. For now, you are assignees. You have no privileges here. You will enter my building and come to this room each day. Do not speak to anyone unless spoken to. Do not venture into other parts of my building. Do not breathe unless I give you express permission to emit that breath. Am I understood?"

The group rises without him issuing an order and I stand, my mouth gaping. I have no idea how to react to this Jackson. He's cold, distant, not at all the Jackson I know.

Though I guess I really don't know him at all.

"There are two elements to our training—internal and external manipulations. We will work on an element of each daily. For today, we will challenge both." He motions to the guard who walks to open the back door. Six more guards enter carrying stacks of wooden circles that look like wheels, each at least five inches in width and fifteen inches in circumference. They sit the stacks in front of us and exit back out the door they came in through. "Women will each take one, men two." We all stare at him, waiting for another command. "Well go on. I don't enjoy repeating myself."

The group steps forward, each of us grabbing our wooden wheels, and then returning to our spots. Jackson starts for the door, and again we wait, but I now know that he expects us to move without him commanding us, so I step out of line to follow him, the others hesitating for only a moment. We make our way back outside and down Gaia Road, the sun bright above us. Jackson points at the wall of flowers that borders all of Triad. "The Healer's Wall was erected years ago to protect Triad from outside threats. Now, it operates as a line between life and death, reminding us that outside our walls, there is nothing, no one, only a dying land. Today, you'll walk that line from the fields to Juniper Gardens."

Murmurs of surprise and worry course through the group.

"But that will take all day," a boy calls.

Jackson turns back for the Vortex. "Then I suggest you get started."

I force myself to head for the wall without looking at Jackson. I don't want anyone to think he would show me any more kindness than the others. Now I know why they were watching us with such curiosity before. Most of these Ancients know Jackson as the next Logean leader. They have probably never seen him act so casually with anyone.

I reach the wall and turn right, the sun beating down above us in violent waves. I wish he would have told me we were doing this today. I would have dressed in lighter clothes, like shorts and a tank instead of pants. I reposition the wheel in my arms, wondering what would happen if I left it here and picked it up when I made it back around.

"Is it true?" a voice asks from behind me and I turn to see a girl rushing up to me. She's smaller than me, just over five foot I would guess, but her arms and legs show strength. "I'm Madison," she says with a small smile.

"I'm—"

"Oh, I know who you are. Everyone does. You're Ari."

I shake my head. "What do you mean? How does everyone know who I am?" I start back down the line of the gate, feeling unsettled. I have a long way to go and don't want to waste any time.

"You came over with J.C. He went back for you. It's really romantic if you ask me."

I stop and look at her. "Jackson and I aren't together. He's…" What exactly?

"See, you call him Jackson. No one calls him *Jackson* except his grandparents."

"Well…" I am at a complete loss on what to say. I don't know J.C. I don't see him as the leader he is. To me, Jackson is…I don't know, more boy, less man, but the longer I'm here, the more I see him with others, the more I realize maybe he was never a boy.

We continue for several minutes in silence, both of us repositioning our wheel from time to time. My biceps have begun to burn already and I wonder how I'll make it all the way around Triad without dropping it or taking a break.

I glance over the wall to a wide sprawl of mountains in the distance. They are dark, haunting, not at all the look of mountains back home.

"That's the Alikaia mountains. They used to have a gate in the wall with a path that led to them, but that was years ago. I don't really remember what they looked like before."

"Before what?"

"Before the water dried up. Before all the trees and grass died. There's nothing there now, just rock."

I eye the mountains as we pass by, curious what else used to exist here on Loge before everything began to die. "So, you don't have much here, huh? Triad, I mean, it's smaller than I imagined."

She considers me for a moment. "We have all we need, I guess. Everything is handmade here, and all our food is grown. And then there are things brought in from the other regions, of course. It's not so bad really."

My eyes travel from the field we're in to the woods just ahead of us. "Do we go through the woods?"

Madison shrugs. "He said to stay with the wall, so I guess. The woods aren't so wide though. We should be through them quickly, and then we'll go past town, past the factories, past the Taking Forest, and then finally to the Juniper Gardens."

"How long do you think it will take?"

Madison grimaces. "All day."

• • •

I slip through the front door of our house so many hours later that I've lost count. It took Madison and me all day, as she had said, to reach the Juniper Gardens, and when we arrived it was so dark I couldn't make out anything but the stars above us and the two giant moons shining down, reminding us of our misery. I was glad Madison walked the wall with me, and by the time we finished, I knew that her mother was a healer, and that she wanted to be a healer, too, but wasn't born with the gift. Her father was pleased when she was assigned to become an RES, he himself one of the many factory workers. She said pride was important in Triad, many working hard and studying to try to evoke some of those skills into their deeper selves in hopes that the healers would pick up on those traits and assign them to RESs or government work.

I sit my wheel down beside one of the chairs in the common room and force myself to go out to the shower, desperate to wash away the day. I let the water run over my face, the water as hot as I can stand it. Once again, I stay there far longer than is likely appropriate, but I don't care. I need the break, the relief. Especially if I'm now supposed to go see Zeus.

I reluctantly make my way out of the shower and to Jackson's room, wishing I could crawl into bed for a few hours of sleep before everything starts again tomorrow, but I know that Zeus is expecting me. I open the door to find Jackson already there, fully dressed, waiting.

"He's expecting us."

I nod.

"I'll just…" He stands and slips past me, causing my cheeks to flush. After today, it's strange to see him so casual.

I change quickly and peek my head out to let him know it's safe to come back inside.

"How are you feeling? I know it's a lot. All assignees are required to walk the wall on the first day. It's sort of a tradition. Something about reminding us what we're fighting for. Anyway, I was going to have you skip it and go see Zeus, but I thought he would get suspicious."

I nod again. Somehow sure that if I speak at all, I'll either complain or cry, so I just sit there, waiting for Jackson to say something else. He doesn't so I just say, "Let's go."

CHAPTER 6

Jackson and I walk the entire way to Zeus's building in silence. We reach the doors and he stops me, my hand midmotion to the door. "Are you sure?"

I smile a little. "It'll be fine," I say, though I know the words are as much for my sake as his. And then for no reason other than the need to feel his strength, I lean in and hug him tightly. "I'll be fine."

Jackson walks me to Zeus's office, hesitates, then dips back to the stairs. He mouths, *I'll be right here*, then closes the door, leaving me alone to face Zeus. I lift my hand to knock just as Zeus's office door opens. "I've been expecting you."

I step inside and take in my surroundings. Dad once told me a wise attack is one where you know your exits. From what I can see there are four doors inside his office, including the one I just came through. I make a mental note that there may be guards stationed outside each of the other doors. Or they could be closets. I had no idea.

Zeus walks over to the wall of windows behind his desk, no doubt the windows Jackson was referring to when we discussed the plan. I feel the gun against my calf, tucked just inside my left boot, and draw a breath. Should I do it now or wait? Zeus presses a hand against the window. It's dark outside, only a few lights in the distance give away that we're in a city. He stays in the same position so long, with me standing a few feet away, neither of us speaking, that I begin to wonder if I'm being tested or if he's expecting someone else to join us. But with each passing second, I feel my heart rate increasing, my nerves twisting into a pretzel. I consider asking about Triad, as Jackson suggested, and then the Operative in me takes over and I reach down for the gun, just as Zeus turns around. I kneel quickly, pretending to adjust the buckle on my boot. Sweat collects on my forehead and I have to draw a quick breath before I stand.

"What are you doing?" Zeus asks as he walks toward me.

I clear my mind, my face of any emotion. "It's taking me some time to get used to your clothes here. They fit differently than what I'm used to."

Zeus considers me. "Take your boots off."

"Sorry?"

He steps closer. "Remove your boots. Now."

"I wasn't aware that you had a no-shoe policy in your office," I say, buying time. If I remove my boots, he'll know. He may already know. I glimpse around at the doors again. I could shoot and run. I'm a solid shot. Even if I can't get a kill shot, I would injure him enough that he wouldn't be able to dial for help, but he could still speak, and if he yelled they would know something happened. Then the healers would get to him before he bled out. An injury shot wouldn't work, it has to kill him.

This processes through my mind in a second, all while I try to maintain my stress-level. Any increases in my levels, and he would interpret my thoughts. I have to keep them shadowed.

Zeus tilts his head to the side and I can tell he's trying to puncture through my thoughts. I'm preparing myself that this is about to get bad and fast, when Zeus's door opens and Jackson comes in, shock on his face. "Oh, I didn't realize you were still meeting." Zeus gives him a look that could make children cry.

"Is there something you need?"

Jackson stands tall, so at ease that if we weren't in such a dire situation I would bow down to his efforts. He's so much better at this than me. "Yes, you've been requested at the Vortex. Another outbreak."

Zeus glances from Jackson to me and back, each second like watching a wild animal preparing to attack its prey. "Very well," he finally says. "We will continue this tomorrow."

I hesitate, unsure if I've been dismissed or what. Jackson nods toward the door for me to go and I start for it, when Zeus calls out. "Tomorrow, no boots."

I am down the stairs and out of his building so fast I feel sure my heart is going to burst out of my chest. I don't stop until I'm back at the house, inside Jackson and my room, my breathing labored. He definitely knew something was up. But did he know what?

Jackson comes through the door a minute later, looking as jarred by the whole thing as me. "Are you all right?" he asks as he places his hands on my face.

"Yes. But he knew something was up, didn't he?"

Jackson sits down on the bed and rakes a hand through his hair, then over his face, before finally glancing up at me. "I don't know. He had guards waiting outside the room. I think he suspected, but he wasn't sure of what exactly. That was close. Too close."

"Was there really an uprising?"

He sighs. "No, but the guard refused to disagree with me in front of Zeus, so he said they had contained it."

I lay back on the bed, allowing my breathing to relax. "Jackson?"

He turns to me. "Yeah?"

"Why are you okay with this? I mean, he's your grandfather."

"You don't know him the way I do. If you did, you'd understand. It's late. We should get some sleep." He shuts out the light and I pull off my boots and place the gun under my pillow. I think back to him at the Vortex, how controlled he was, how you could tell they wanted to impress him.

"What?" he asks. I hadn't realized I was staring at him.

"You were unbelievable today," I admit, embarassed to say it out loud. "The way they responded to you, respected you. I had no idea…"

He slumps against his pillow on the floor. "It's the name, Ari, not me."

I lean over the side of the bed, holding his gaze. "No. It was you, all you." I lay back down before I give away just how enthralled I'd been with him. I fumble with my covers, my eyes on the ceiling. "So, what now? We try again tomorrow?"

"No. We come up with a new plan."

CHAPTER 7

The next day, Jackson walks me to the Panacea for a required check with Emmy before RES training. He doesn't mention Zeus all morning, and I find myself wishing we would talk about the new plan already so I could stop worrying about it.

I notice the other Ancients watching us as we walk along the path that borders the Cutana River, and I find myself wishing I would have asked to go there alone. I don't want the others to assume he's going easier on me, not because I'm worried about how they'll view me. I don't want to jeopardize the respect they have for him.

Emmy and I walk out the back of the Panacea and down the back steps into the Juniper Gardens below. Jackson left at Emmy's insistence that she needed to observe me on her own, which at first made me nervous, but now I'm grateful.

In front of us is nothing but row after row of flowers that smell so sweet they hit me like a spray of perfume the moment we near. To the far left I can see the factories that make everything we use for daily life. And then to the right I spy what I had been most curious about since coming to Loge. It is a forest full of trees, all the same size and shape, all perfectly spaced. A wooden sign stands post at the front of each row, each with a number on it, though from this distance I can't make out what the numbers are or determine what they might represent. I know what the forest is without having to ask.

"Those are Taking trees, aren't they?" I motion to the forest, curious what it would have looked like just before the Ancients came to Earth to Take. The trees function as hyperspaces between Earth and Loge, which allowed the Ancients to travel between planets during the Taking. I imagine Ancients lined up in their designated rows, disappearing into the trees like magic. Now, it reminds me of a closed store back home, dark and lonely, desperate to be open for business.

Emmy nods. "That the Taking Forest, though it not been used in some weeks now. Zeus have it monitored."

I remembered Madison mentioning it yesterday, but it was dark when we passed and I was too tired at that point to care. "What is that beside it?" I ask, pointing to the fenced in square structure to the right of the forest. It is smaller than the houses here, but no more than ten or so Ancients could fit inside. It has the texture of wood, but the sun reflects off it as though it were metal.

"That the Earthly port. It link to the main ports on Earth."

My pulse speeds up. "You mean that takes you to Earth? Is it operational?"

Emmy gives me a concerned look. "It dangerous, child. Guarded all day, every day."

I see what she means. Standing just inside the fence are two guards, both armed. "Right," I say, but inside my mind is churning. Two guards. That's nothing. I could—

Emmy stops, her expression serious. "Not here."

"I wasn't—"

"Not here," she repeats.

"Okay." I follow Emmy down the center path that cuts

through the Juniper Gardens, forcing my thoughts to remain on the scenery—and not on the plan already developing in my mind.

The flowers are wilder looking than the ones back home. No petunias or roses. These are huge with flowing petals, all rich with vibrant colors—deep purples and bright pinks and yellows that rival the sun. I stare up into the sky and smile. Jackson had said the sky was purple and he was right, though the simple description doesn't do it justice. The sky is a very faint lavender mixed with teal blue, so it looks more like something someone painted than a reality in front of me. There are clouds in the sky, but very few and the ones that are there are wispy. For the most part it is a clear, beautiful day. The sun is present, as it is on Earth, and that similarity brings me tremendous comfort, even though I know I'm staring at a different sun than ours.

"How you feel, child?" Emmy asks, and now that I've met several Ancients, I wonder why her accent is different. Most of the others sound like me, but Emmy sounds as though the language is new for her.

She chuckles lightly behind me. "We hear you too, child," she says, motioning to her ear. "We hear much more than that device of yours detects."

I turn to her, studying her to see if I can feel anything from her, but all I see is the same wrinkled woman in front of me and no emotions or stress moving from her to me. "Why can't I feel you, Emmy?" I ask, hoping I don't sound rude.

"It's not our way. We see you. No one sees us." She gestures further down the path. "Walk with me. I rarely get to walk."

I nod my head and she takes my hand, shaking it lightly in hers, a smile on her face. Her demeanor is so different out here, not at all concerned or riddled with fear as I remember her from earlier. Finally, the path we're on dead ends into another path that runs perpendicular to it. Emmy halts beside me and I look over to find her head high, her expression now morose.

"Emmy…?" I follow her gaze straight ahead to the dark and ashy land beyond the wall. , "How does that happen, Emmy?" I ask, shocked at how the gardens, so beautiful, can lead to something so sad.

She draws a breath. "That what happens to us if we stay here." Her hand twitches in mine and for the briefest second I feel her emotions—worry and sadness run through her.

She reaches out to the tip of a dying flower on the wall in front us. In its younger day, I imagine it was a deep blue or maybe violet. Now, it's brown and yellow and every other shade of death. I expect Emmy to pluck it from the wall, pruning as I've seen my mom do so many times in our yard, but instead she closes her eyes, cradling the flower so she's barely touching it. Then suddenly, the brown in the flower's petals recedes, replaced by a vivid yellow. The wrinkled and broken stem straightens and twists until it looks like a freshly grown flower, young and beautiful, without the slightest imperfection.

I'm in awe.

"So it's true…" I whisper.

Emmy tilts her head. "We the reason we live." She turns to me, her hand still in mine. "Twenty-five of us responsible for an entire species. But we dying, child. And there are no more born."

I realize she isn't telling me all of this to be informative. "What can I do, Emmy? What are you asking me to do?"

Her expression turns urgent and she jerks me toward her roughly, again shocking me with her strength. Her face is inches from mine, her eyes wild, as she says, "Get us off this planet."

I shake my head, at a loss for how she could think I could do anything. "But…how? I'm not—how?" I study her eyes, searching for anything that could give me hope because I want to go home more than I want anything else in the world.

She steps back. "You find a way. I see it in you. I see strength and"—she tilts her head again, squinting up at me as though she's trying to figure out a complex puzzle—"plus something else. You special, child. I feel it. And soon you feel it, too."

She turns back to the wall and takes out the set of beads she keeps in her pocket, running them through her fingertips again and again as she walks from flower to flower, healing those that are less than perfect.

I replay what she's told me, hoping to find something in what she said that gives a deeper explanation. The planet is dying, that much is clear. Beyond the beautiful wall in front of me is nothing but rock, leaving no hope of life. I don't know what to do. I don't know how I can help.

All I know is that the look on Emmy's face said one thing— Loge is dying and we're running out of time.

• • •

I don't wait for Jackson to come back for me. Instead, wanting time to myself, I walk out of the Panacea and take the path that runs along the river. A few Ancients pass me on the way, and each studies me with curiosity. I keep my head even and my expression blank, not wanting to engage them, not now when I have no idea what I'm doing and all I can think about is how I'm supposed to kill their leader.

I reach Jackson's house—my house—and slip inside and to our room without seeing any of the others. I have twenty minutes before I need to be at the Vortex for RES training, and I want to take the time to think. I go into the kitchen for some water. It's kept in a circular dispenser beside the refrigerator, along with various different fruity extracts that I could drop into the water to give it flavor. I'm examining the various different packets, when Vill sits down at the bar in the kitchen, his handiwork etched into every inch of the wood.

"Ari, can we chat?"

I turn to face him, nervous, though he doesn't give off any peculiar vibes. I wonder if he's controlling his feelings or if he keeps his true feelings guarded all the time. Or maybe, he's just so mellow that no hint of emotion ever creeps into his aura. "Sure. We didn't get a chance to talk much last night. I love your work," I say, motioning around the kitchen. The walls are a continuous painting of grass growing at different stages. It's a little strange, except for the detail, which is impeccable. He shows a healer pressing her palms into the earth and then as though on a reel, the scenes change around the room until the final scene is nothing but a valley of green grass.

He scratches his head, looking uncomfortable again at my mentioning his work. "Thanks. I can't really help it. It's a part of me, like breathing."

I nod. "I can imagine." My eyes drift around the room and then back to him when I realize he's waiting for me to look at him.

"Just like Jackson."

"Sorry, what's just like Jackson?"

Vill leans back in his stool, lacing his fingers in front of him as he releases a long breath. "You don't know him. You might think you do, but you don't. Not the way I do." He holds up his hands at the expression on my face. "And I'm not saying that in a threatening way. I'm saying that so you understand that he is what he has been ingrained to be. Sure, he fights it. Sure, he wants to be different. But he can't change that tick inside him, no more than I could stop painting or sculpting. No easier than you could stop leading."

At this I take a step back. "Leading? What? And I don't know what you're talking about. What tick inside him?"

Vill ignores my last question. "You *are* a leader, Ari. You were born a leader and you will die a leader. It is who you are.

Everyone who meets you knows it. And you know it, even if you question it. You react like a leader, thinking ahead of time so you know your actions are properly directed." He stops to watch me, and I know I must look uncomfortable. I feel uncomfortable. This isn't at all the conversation I thought we would be having. I look away and then down at my feet.

"I used to be a leader. Now, I'm…I don't know what I am."

"You'll find yourself again. Before you know it, you will be leading again. But you need to first see Jackson, really see him, for who he is, instead of what you thought he was or who you now believe him to be."

My eyes drift up to his. "To be honest, I don't know how I see him now." I think of the boy I knew on Earth, and now the man I see here. I can't make the two fit together.

"Then do me a favor. Try to imagine what it would be like to be petrified to think or act freely. Not just worried that you will disappoint, but literally afraid that you or someone you love would die if you ever thought or acted of your own accord. That has been Jackson's life. So before you start judging him for not telling you who he is, maybe you should consider his motives and consider that perhaps, for someone like him, he put everything on the line for you too and you pushed him away."

I open my mouth to respond, but no words come out. My life is built on simplicity—truth or lies, right or wrong— so much so that it's impossible for me to imagine a gray area. That maybe someone could lie and it could be righteous, or someone could do wrong and that could be brave. I can't wrap my mind around it.

Vill gives me a half smile. "Think about it."

"I will," I say, realizing that if Vill knew me on anything close to the same level he knows Jackson, then he would know he gave me no choice but to think about it. Because now, I'm left wondering if I know Jackson at all.

I'm about to slip out of the kitchen, when Jackson rushes into the house, never stopping to look at us. Vill and I exchange worried looks and both follow Jackson down the hall and to our room.

"Are you all right?" Vill asks from the open doorway.

Jackson jerks his shirt over his head, exposing his bare chest, and tosses it in a rumpled mess into the corner. "Oh, you know, same old. I'm over at my grandparents—visiting Mami— when he comes home. He of course accuses her of being too easy on me and they get into an argument, which she quickly admits her wrongdoing and apologizes, then he sends her to her room like she's a child. I can't stand it. I hate him. I *hate* him." He yanks on his hair and drops his arms in a long, defeated sign. And that's when his eyes find mine. He hadn't realized I was there. "Great. Thanks. I thought we talked about this." He shoots Vill an annoyed look, then says to me, "He's requested to see you. You're skipping RES training today. We have ten minutes," before shutting the door in our faces.

I take a step back, my mind reeling. In all my time with Jackson, I have never once felt he acted his age, instead always appearing together and organized. He has a demeanor that says he feels childishness is beneath him, especially here, where he exhibits control over others. But this…this was like watching a little boy unravel.

Vill nods toward his room and shuts the door quietly behind us. The room is like an explosion of Vill-ness. The walls are all carved or painted. The floor has splattering of paint here and there, all different shades, all likely belonging to a different project. "See what I mean," he says to me, motioning to a chair in the corner of the room for me to sit. It's an animal of some sort, with the head of a lion as the back and giant wings as the arm rests. A cushion covers the wood in the seat area and as I near I realize it's handmade as well.

The words, "One world, one being," are sewn into the top of the cushion.

"Why did he get upset at you?" I say as I sit in the chair.

Vill grabs a tiny figurine and a knife from his dresser and begins whittling away at it. "He doesn't want you to know how bad it is. How can he pretend to protect you if he can't even protect his grandmother? He doesn't want you to view him as weak. I tried to talk to him about it, but he won't listen."

I'm about to ask him more, when Jackson's door bursts open and he starts calling my name, aggravation in his voice. I jump up and rush out of Vill's room, narrowly stopping myself from slamming into him. "Hey. I was in Vill's room. Everything okay?"

He shakes his head, glaring behind me at Vill. "Perfect. Now, if you two are done, we need to leave. He's not one to appreciate waiting." And with that, he storms down the hall without another glance my way.

CHAPTER 8

"Please, have a seat," Zeus says, motioning to one of two chairs in front of him. He remains standing, which makes the whole thing all that more awkward.

Jackson refused to talk to me the entire walk here except to say that depending upon what Zeus wanted, I may miss all of RES training today. We left in such a rush, I didn't have a chance to grab the gun, and we have yet to discuss the new plan. I wanted to question him, force him to tell me what to do, but

the moment we stepped onto Zeus's floor, Jackson was taken to another room, while I was brought here to see Zeus. I eye the chairs, not wanting to lower myself to sitting while he towers over me. Zeus likes power and control. For him to make others sit while he walks around them is no doubt yet another way for him to show his superiority to anyone who enters his office. I don't play those games.

I cross my arms. "Thank you for the invitation, but I would rather stand." Immediately my thoughts go to what Jackson said about his grandmother, and I find myself getting angry with Zeus on her behalf. No one should be treated that way, especially not his wife. The entire thing makes me feel sick. And that's when I realize Zeus's stare has turned lethal, his back tense. He knows what I was thinking, but instead of growing angrier, his lips pull together in the tiniest of smiles and he says, "Very well, stand," as though he were expecting me to say just that. "I see you have appropriately forgotten your boots today." The smile widens, and I have to draw a breath to keep my stress level in check. He knew. How did he know?

Zeus walks over to the wall of windows in the far left wall that overlook all of Triad. From this vantage point you can see everything in motion—the shops, the people, everything and everyone as busy as ants building a colony. I imagine to Zeus they are ants, tiny useless things that are of no consequence and have no brainpower beyond what propels them through the day.

"You lack self control unlike anyone I have ever encountered," Zeus says. "I imagined you to be quite disciplined. And I suppose in ways you are. But your mind, it's a constant, ravenous creature that lacks precision and grace. We will need to right that problem before you take post."

"And what post is that exactly?"

He turns, the hint of a smile again on his face. "As an RES. Of course."

I get the impression he isn't telling me everything. "Is that why you wanted me to become an Ancient? So I could become one of your RES?"

He tilts his head in thought. "I have long since felt the human plan would involve an airborne tactic. It became useful for me to create more of us than of you. And so yes, I ordered the healings, particularly for some of you."

"What do you mean 'some of you'?"

"You will see, I am sure. Of course, you were healed for personal reasons. Your father has forever denied coexistence for Ancients. How very ironic that his only child is now one of them." I start to defend Dad, when his head jerks and he blurts, "Ironic: Happening in the opposite way to what is expected."

"Why do you do that?" I ask, realizing that my abrasiveness is what annoys him the most. The best way to keep him where I want him is to push it to the max.

He gives a half laugh and walks over to his desk, dropping a tiny brown circle from a wooden bowl into his mouth. "You are the first to ever ask. Can you believe that?"

"Yes. I can. Most fear you."

"Ah, fear. Humans call it respect. There is no difference."

"You're not answering my question."

"Indeed." He hesitates for a moment then says, "I was the test subject for the transmitter that allows RESs to sense stress. I wanted to know exactly what it felt like, and in my haste, I requested the first trial be made on me. As it sits, it altered my mind in ways the healers cannot undo."

For a moment I almost respect his choice. Choosing to test the transmitter on himself instead of his staff could be viewed as brave, would be viewed as brave, if I were talking to anyone other than Zeus.

He fixes his gaze on me, the piercing silver look that has always left me with chills, but I no longer worry over angering him. I'm somehow sure that he won't kill me. At least not yet.

"What is your plan for the other humans? Are they part of your army now, too?"

Zeus goes back to the window, his focus on something far away. "No. They are not part of my army. They will fight *for* us, not with us. Now, that is enough for today." And as though he spoke an order to someone waiting, the door opens to his office and a healer walks in. I can tell by the way she's dressed in the same shapeless smock as Emmy and the others at the Panacea, though she looks much younger, middle aged, where I would call Emmy almost elderly.

"This way," she says, and I glance from Zeus to her, unsure of who she's speaking to.

Zeus turns, the half smile returning to his face. "Your analysis begins today. Should your brain resist—as I suspect it will—you will come again and again to the blue room until you surrender. I told you when you arrived that I would break you. Today, prepare to receive the first crack."

For a split second, I want to run. I want to run as far away as I can and hide. But there is nowhere to hide here, no one to shield me. And so I do what I have been taught to do—I go, prepared to face whatever he can throw at me. Besides, I was trained by my dad, one of the most ruthless trainers to exist. How bad can the blue room really be?

The healer leads me to the stairs and down a floor to a room that feels like an isolation chamber—like the Ancient testing chambers back home, where they tortured Ancients just to discover the best way to kill them. The walls and floor and ceiling are all glaringly white, almost reflective. The healer doesn't enter the room with me. Instead, she shuts me inside, and I walk around the empty square area, studying the walls as though I can find something in them that tells me why this room is called the blue room. After several seconds, I realize there is nothing here, only the white and me. I walk to the center of the room, waiting for instruction, and then a blue beam shoots down from the ceiling into the space beside me, then another and another until ten beams of blue light encircle me. I press my hand forward, but I'm unable to reach outside the blue, the beams like bars, caging me in. The bars begin to move, spinning around me, and then a bright white light shines down over me, through me. I have to force myself to draw deep, settling breaths because I can feel my heart hitting in my chest, warning me of danger.

And that's when I hear the healer's voice. *Calm your mind,* she says. Not from a speaker or somewhere in the room, but in my mind. The realization is so unsettling that I grab my head with my hands, eager to push her out.

Settle down, child.

"What are you doing to me?"

My name is Lydian.

"What do you do?"

I torture.

The words churn through me, sending chills down my spine. I clear my throat. "I can take whatever you plan to do."

"We shall see. I will ask you a question, then project images into your mind, one after another until you supply the answer," Lydian says, this time aloud.

I steady my gaze on her. "Whenever you're ready."

"Where is the entrance?"

What? What entrance? "I have no idea what you're talking about."

"Very well."

What entrance? I pick my brain apart, searching for random conversations, anything, that she could be talking about, and come up empty. I would never tell her, regardless, but it's unsettling to think she knows something that's happening on Earth and I don't.

I ready myself for whatever she might throw at me. It's just an image after all. An image. What she doesn't tell me is that the room will project the image from my mind onto the walls, the ceiling, all around me, then suddenly the spinning stops. I'm in a dark room, a single lamp offering the only light. I inch further into the room, my senses telling me that something is wrong there, very wrong. I push open a door in the back of the room and see Gretchen, my best friend, tied to a chair, her right arm strapped to a table beside her. A man stands before her, hunching down so they are eye to eye. He asks her a question, but I can't hear the words, all I hear is Gretchen's breathing, ragged and afraid.

The man asks the question again, and then slices off her pinky finger.

She screams out, I scream out. And then suddenly I realize, with horror, that this might be really happening. Someone could have Gretchen, torturing her, until I answer instead of torturing me. No, she's on Earth. Jackson said she's on Earth.

Beads of sweat drop down my back as I try to push the image away, close my eyes, block it out, but there is no escaping it. My mind can only see.

The man presses down on Gretchen's wound and speaks again. This time she cries back, and I can tell by the way her mouth moves that she's screaming, "I don't know, I don't know." The man steps away from her, speaks again, and then slices off the rest of her fingers. I feel my legs go weak below me, nausea swirling through my stomach. I reach out and something shocks me back into place.

Where is the entrance? A voice says to me, and I'm yanked from the scene, back in the blueroom, but I'm no longer standing. I'm kneeled on the ground, my cheeks wet from tears I hadn't realized I'd spilt.

I glance up at Lydian. "I don't know."

Zeus joins her in the glass room, his look some combination of curiosity and annoyance. "That will do for today," he says, and the blue beams around me disappear. He leans in closer to the glass, his eyes so close to madness that I wonder if he's on something. "You will do well to remember where you are, who you are, else I will see to it that you are destroyed. You will tell me where to find the entrance." He starts for the door.

I push to my feet. "I'm not afraid of dying." The words slip out before I can catch them.

Zeus turns back, a devlish grin on his face. "It isn't your life I would take. No, I will slowly take the lives of everyone you know until you are alone, begging for death."

CHAPTER 9

I wait until Zeus and Lydian are both long gone before leaving the blue room. I don't want them to see how shaken he's made me. I don't want to admit that I'm afraid. I close the door, just as Jackson exits a door across from mine. He doesn't notice me at first, and I'm about to call out to him, when he slumps against the wall, his head in his hands. He mumbles something to himself, and I see a dark gray aura swirling over him. He's completely off his guard and he's never off guard. I watch him, knowing I should let him know I'm there or do something to help, but I'm in a trance, mesmerized by how someone can act so in control but inside be so…gone. Finally, he kicks away from the door and hescans the room before landing on me.

"Ari…" he says. "I was just…"

I shake my head and meet him in the middle of the open foyer. "Me, too," I say, hoping he knows what I mean, that he doesn't have to explain. If his last hour was anything like mine, I get it. And now I feel more than ever that Vill is right. Maybe the Jackson I thought I knew is really nothing close to who he is and maybe the real Jackson is everything I had hoped he would be.

I link my hand into his, as friends because that's what we are, and we leave Zeus's building without talking. It isn't until we're outside that I glance down and notice the bottom of his shirt is smeared in blood. I scan his face, his arms, his hands, but there is no sign of a cut or wound. Where was the blood from? Reaching out to touch the shirt, my eyes lift to his. "Are you all right?" I ask.

His glance drops to the shirt and his teeth grit together. "Perfect. It's part of my training. Zeus's plan to mold me into a ruler, but really what he wants is for me to become a carbon copy of him." He looks up, his eyes searching mine. "But I can't do that. I could never be like him."

"I know," I say. "Look, we don't have to talk about what happened if you don't want. I know my side was nothing I want to rehash, and I'm no where near as important to Zeus as you." At this Jackson laughs sarcastically. "What I'm trying to say is, we don't have to talk about the bad stuff…if you don't want to. As long as you promise to tell me if it gets to be too much. And I'll do the same."

His body relaxes a little as he takes me in. "You're okay with that? I mean, after everything, I thought you wanted full disclosure."

I tug on his hand and we start back walking down the main street of Triad. "I want you to tell me the important stuff. I want you to trust me enough to tell me the important stuff. But I don't want you to relive something horrible just so I know what's going on. Trust me, I've experienced enough in training to know that not everything needs to be discussed. I just want to make sure you're okay." As soon as the words leave me I wish I could take them back. Not because they're untrue, but because it hints at feelings I'm not ready to explore.

"Okay." Jackson smiles a bit as he squints up at the sun. "Are you hungry? We can grab something to eat back home.

And speaking of eating, how was your visit with Emmy?"

I grin up at him. "So food makes you think of Emmy, huh? Is she a good cook or something?"

He laughs. "Probably, but I wouldn't know. She's a healer, so I automatically think of them when I think about food."

I remember what Emmy told me and how she made the dying flower come back to life. I wonder if she can do that for people, too. I find Jackson watching me and realize I've waited too long to answer his question, and feel torn between telling him the full truth or part of what Emmy told me. Sighing, I decide that if I expect him to be honest with me, then I need to be equally honest with him. "Emmy told me there are very few healers left and if we can't get off Loge soon, we're all going to die as quickly as the rest of your planet."

He considers what I've told him for a long time before replying. "She asked for your help?"

"Yes."

His face crinkles up like it does when he's worried or in deep thought. "That's not good."

"Why? I was actually wondering if she could help us with our plan. I don't know how yet, but watching her work life back into the plants in Juniper Garder made me wonder if that ability could be used...for other things."

Jackson looks over at me, his expression full of alarm. "I don't know. The healers don't ask for help, they give it. For her to ask..." He trails off, deep in thought as we make our way back into the house. "I need to think. I'm going to grab a shower. Meet you back out here in fifteen?"

"Where are we going?"

He glances at me. "We're going to see Cybil." Then he turns and is gone out the back door before I can ask why he's suddenly so rattled.

I decide to go change before leaving. I may not be bleeding like Jackson, but I still feel overwhelmed and exhausted from my torture session with Lydian. I head to Jackson and my room and slip inside, instantly feeling more relaxed. Something about being away from everyone else, behind closed doors, brings comfort. I sift through the clothes in our closet and spot Jackson's shirt in a pile on the floor. I glance back out into the room and listen for any hint of incoming footsteps. Once I'm sure it's safe, I flip the shirt inside out and hold it in front of me, examining each inch to see where the concentration of blood could have come from. The front is all but clean, only showing a splotch of blood here or there, but then I turn it over to the back and my mouth drops open. There are splotches of red all over the shirt, some darker than others, and the inside bottom of the shirt is so red it no longer looks like a blue T-shirt at all.

I slump back into the chair beside the closet with the shirt still held tight in my hands. What happened to him back there? And why wouldn't he tell me? This is different than hiding something from me. This is a means of protection, like he's trying to shield me from whatever horror awaits him each day with Zeus. But I don't want to be shielded. I want to help him or comfort him or do whatever he needs to let him know that it's okay; he doesn't have to be strong all the time.

After returning the shirt to its crumpled position on the floor, I pick out another pair of black pants and a long sleeve black T-shirt, before going to the bathroom to splash water on my face. I stare at my reflection as I pat my face dry, not seeing myself at all, only the blood on Jackson's shirt and what it suggests. If Zeus is willing to torture Jackson, what would he do to the humans here?

Suddenly a sick feeling circles through my stomach, and I'm out of the bathroom and back to my room, eager to question Jackson about what I'm about to see. But as I step into our room, my thoughts cut short. Jackson is already there, and I find myself stuck, watching, as he slips on a shirt similar to the tanks the Landings boys back home used to wear in the warmer months. He smiles up at me and brushes his wet hair out of his face with his hand. I'd forgotten how unbelievably fit he is, and it's a strange thing to see him looking so strong and healthy, when just a while ago he looked like a broken little boy. I feel something tug in my stomach as I lift my eyes to his, some pull that instantly wants to protect him from whatever has him so afraid.

His smile slowly fades as he watches me. "Don't do that. Not you. Don't stare at me like I'm some mental case. I don't care what Vill told you—I'm fine."

And the look on his face, like he's somehow convinced himself of this or that he's repeating something that's been told to him again and again is enough to pull me from my trance. I grab his bloody shirt from the floor. "Yeah, because this looks fine."

"It was from training. I told you that. It isn't the first time I've left there bloody, and don't tell me that you never once left your trainings with a little blood on your shirt."

I flip the shirt inside out and toss it at him. "This isn't a little blood. What did he do to you, huh? Why won't you tell me? Why won't you let me help?"

Jackson straightens. "This has nothing to do with you, that's why. And I can handle it. I have always handled it, and I don't need you or anyone else getting involved."

"That's not the point. You don't have to handle it on your own. After everything we've been through, haven't you at least figured that out? We don't have to do this on our own. We can lean on each other, help each other. We can be there for—"

His releases a sarcastic laugh. "Yeah, because you're just dying to be there for me, right? Was that before or after you agreed to be just friends?"

"I—"

"It doesn't matter. We need to go." He starts for the door, and then turns back with a sad smile. "I want you. In every way. In any way I can get you. And if that means being your friend, then that's what I'll be. But don't expect me to open up about the worst parts of my life when I am next to nothing to you now."

"Jackson…" I look away, wondering how the conversation turned south so quickly. I still can't look at him when I speak, my voice so small that I'm not sure he can even hear me. "I want to trust you. Every fiber in my body aches to trust you. But…"

"Yeah, I know. You can't." He sighs loudly. "As I said, it doesn't matter, and we've got someplace to be. So if you're ready…" He rakes a hand through his hair and then over his face, and all I can do is nod because I have absolutely no idea what else to say. Surely he knows how this feels for me, too. It isn't like my feelings just disappeared, which makes it all that much harder to watch him in pain knowing I can't comfort him, not in the way I want.

I take a deep breath and follow Jackson outside, glad for the open air. Somehow intense emotions feel less empowering in the open. We walk back around the residences and cross the second bridge to the Vortex. I want to grab his hand, but I know that's too much to ask of him right now, so I stare straight ahead, fighting my inner self to stay quiet, to keep my thoughts in check. I crack one knuckle after the other, and then glance over at Jackson just as he shakes his head in frustration.

"What?" he asks.

"Are you all right?"

He slows his pace. "Do you remember your first training with your dad?"

"I…" I fall silent at the look on his face, distant and angry, and say only, "Yes."

"I remember mine with Zeus, too. I was five years old and he was testing my reflexes, tossing stuff around the room for me to grab before it hit the ground. He was so proud of me that he forced Mami to come watch us practice. Even to this day, that's the best memory I have of him. Back then, he was kind. He would never have treated Mami or me the way he does now. But everything has changed—his mind, his outlook, even the way he carries himself is different, like he's waiting for someone to deceive him. And right now, the person he trusts least on Loge…is you." We've stopped halfway over the bridge, the crystal water below swooshing against the bank. "So, yeah, don't expect me to rope you further into Zeus's madness. You've got enough of it with what everyone else is asking you to do." "I'm not afraid of him," I finally say, knowing the words are only half true, but I'll never admit to fearing him, not when I know how much he enjoys invoking fear in others. I won't give him that satisfaction.

Jackson starts back over the bridge. "I know, but just because you aren't afraid doesn't mean there isn't a reason to be afraid."

"Are you afraid of him?" I ask, knowing I'm treading in the danger zone of too personal information.

He stiffens. "Completely. But I'm not afraid of him hurting me. I'm afraid of him hurting others, those I care about. He's like that, Ari. He will kill someone you love just to watch you squirm."

I think to what Zeus said back in the blueroom, about how he would kill everyone I love. Silence settles over us, my mind on the impossible tasks set before me.

We enter the Vortex and head down a spiral set of stairs to the left. "You need to prepare yourself, okay? Lots of these people are still being acclimated, and as you can imagine, Zeus's form of acclimation isn't exactly humane. Just prepare yourself."

"You act like you're worried I might do something extreme."

"Just try to behave. Remember, Zeus sees all. Don't give him a reason to hurt these people."

"Okay." I swallow hard, as he opens the first door on the right and waits for me to step inside. The door leads to a wide set of stairs that drop down forever into a void of bright light. The stairs themselves are rough and cracked, as though they've been used many times and hardly maintained. I glance over at Jackson. "This way I'm guessing?"

"Just remember what I said," he whispers, before starting down the steps. I stare after him, worried about what I'm going to see. For Jackson to be this concerned over my reaction it must be bad—very bad. I prepare myself for injured or sedated people, something that suggests they're being mistreated, but when I drop to the bottom of the stairs, I see only dozens of curtained rooms, like the ones at the Panacea. Most have the curtains open and as we pass by each, I peek inside, again expecting something startling, but I'm almost more shocked by the normalcy. A pair of boys sits at a table in the first room playing a game on a small table. An older woman sleeps quietly in her bed in the second room. We pass more and more rooms, each with humans inside and not one of them acts in any way afraid.

"I thought you said they were being acclimated?"

"They are," Jackson says. "These have already acclimated. The others are this way." He goes through a set of double doors at the end of the hall and instantly it feels like we've entered a completely different building. Just like the previous room, this one is lined with rooms shielded by curtains, but here all the curtains are closed and there's no sound from inside the rooms except the occasional beeping. I turn back to Jackson. "Is Cybil here?"

He nods. "Yes, I'm hoping she's better. Maybe she can help us." He stops in front of one of the rooms, and I jerk open the curtain to see Cybil sitting on her bed. Her head has been shaved, her skin so pale it's almost transparent. Deep circles shadow her eyes. "What have they done to you?" I whisper. She holds something in her hand she seems to be trying to open, but each time she grabs the clasp her hands begin to shake so violently she drops the tiny thing into her lap and has to start all over again.

My mind flashes to the first time I saw her, when Dad introduced her as my new trainer. She was the very image of what an Engineer should be—confident and sharp, from her pinned back black hair to her pressed uniform, everything about her on that day oozed leadership. I remember how she looked me in the eye every time she spoke to me, just like any respectable Operative. Now, she's yet to look up. I'm not even sure she realizes we're here.

"Cybil?" I say as I sit down on the edge of her bed. She snatches the trinket and backs up against her headboard, her eyes wide with fear. "It's okay. It's me, Ari. Do you remember me?" The whole thing is so pitiful that I wish I could give her a hug, but I know that would be too much for her right now. Finally after a long moment, I reach out my hand, like you would when trying to pet an animal for the first time. "Cybil, it's Ari. Ari Alexander."

"Alexander? Alexander!" She rises onto her knees and edges toward me. "Alexander, Alexander. I'm supposed to… no wait…I can't remember. I can't…" She cups her arms around her head and begins to sway from right to left. "Why can't I remember? What have they done to me? No memory. Alexander." Her eyes flash up to mine and she's in my face before I can respond. "I know that name."

Jackson takes a step toward us and I toss up my hand to stop him. She needs to know that I'm not afraid of her, that I'm a friend. "Yes," I say, holding her gaze. "I'm Ari Alexander. You were my trainer."

She slumps back onto the bed, her legs crossed in front of her. "No, that's not right. That's not why I'm here."

"Okay, so why are you here? Do you know?"

Cybil lowers her voice. "I'm here for Alexander." And then as though someone could hear her, two female Ancients enter the room, both wearing all white. Cybil cowers at seeing them and pushes herself off the bed and into the corner of the room. "No. I didn't mean it. I won't say anything else. Please don't—" And then before she can continue, one of the Ancients braces Cybil while the other injects something into her arm.

I step forward, but Jackson gently holds me back. "Don't," he says. "They're just trying to relax her. Her levels are too high. Look." He points to a monitor beside her bed, where sure enough her heart rate is off the charts. Still, I can't handle seeing Cybil, someone I have always known as so strong, looking so weak. I edge closer to them, shaking Jackson off.

"Is that necessary?" I ask.

One of them turns to me, her expression full of genuine concern. "Unfortunately, she has been unstable since coming here. We fear her mind isn't processing where she is or what's happening. She keeps talking about a mission and then her eyes dart around as though she's said too much. A few others have had issues adjusting as well, but nothing like this. And her progress isn't improving."

The other female has Cybil back in her bed, and the sight is almost enough to make me want to cry. She's curled up in a ball, shaking so violently the frame rattles against the wall behind her. I don't know how this could happen to someone so completely in control. This isn't Cybil. She's strong. She's intelligent. She's—

My eyes snap up from the floor and back to Cybil, scrutinizing her body, her face, her eyes. Her lips twitch just a touch—hardly noticeable, unless you're trained to notice things, like me, which she knows. I watch her for another long moment, while the Ancients run more tests. Her expression is completely blank, almost catatonic. But she smiled, I know it. The Cybil I know is fiercely smart and her job back home was Special Ops Assistant to Dad. I remember when she brought me to the viewing lab, with all its T-screens trained on Latent Ancients on Earth. She has spent most of her career watching the Latent Ancients blend in to our world. Plus, she worked directly for Dad. Is it possible that she's here on some mission from him? If so, it's entirely possible that she's faking all of this. She's smart enough to do it. But then why would she pretend in front of me? Unless…

I spin around, surveying the room, searching for some sign of a camera, but find nothing. Maybe they have other ways of monitoring the room or maybe their cameras are smaller. Regardless, Cybil would never let on what she's doing while she's being watched.

Jackson touches my arm. "Are you all right?"

I nod, returning my attention to Cybil. "Perfect. Is she allowed to leave the room? I think she might do better if she were outside and allowed to see where she is."

He cocks an eyebrow at me, so I let all my thoughts move from me to him, hoping they are clear. His eyes shift from suspicion to understanding. "Not yet. They won't allow her to leave. But you can visit her. Maybe that would help." He lifts a finger to his mouth and then his ear before discreetly motioning around the room. So they are listening to what we say. That's fine. I can play this game.

"Great." I walk over to Cybil and bend down until we are face to face. "I'm coming back tomorrow. I plan to help you." The words are innocent enough, but Cybil's eyes instantly brighten. She understands what I'm saying. Maybe I'm not alone in this after all. Confidence grows within me, and for the first time, I allow the reality of what I'm about to do set in.

I'm going to kill Zeus.

CHAPTER 10

Jackson and I walk back through the Vortex in silence. I can hear the RES assignees training behind the double doors, and I wonder what they're doing, if Madison is in there.

"Should I go on to RES training?" I ask.

Jackson shakes his head. "Not today. It's almost over now, anyway. I'll make sure you're caught up for tomorrow."

We walk the rest of the way to our house in silence, the sight of Cybil making me so homesick it hurts.

I remember the very first day of Field Training, or F.T., like it happened only moments ago. Gretchen and I went into the gym, both of us so nervous we refused to talk. The gym had nothing in it on that day and it was huge, so, so huge. We had never been inside the gym as it was restricted for F.T. use only, but every day you could hear what went on inside. Occasionally Gretchen and I would stop by the doors to listen in to what they were doing, and then we'd pretend we were in there and she'd say, "I can totally master limits. No problem." And she'd go into some spiel about the mental mechanics of limits and how all you have to do is train your brain to know that it's a simulation. I'd half listen to her as they started up combat training, because combat was always my favorite. I wanted to prove, even at a very young age, that I was tough, but on that day—our first day of F.T.—all that toughness was pushed to the very back of my mind, replaced by worry and fear. It was one thing to train with Dad, a complete other to face my fellow classmates or, worse, Operatives.

Gretchen and I took our seats on the floor with the other twenty-three F.T. students. Looking back, I thought nothing of Jackson, who even then must have been traveling back and forth from Loge to Earth, even then an RES. I didn't know he would be the opponent he grew to be or that he would be my greatest rival for top seed—something that seems so stupid to me now. I knew he was smart. Grades were always announced after every test, something intended by our professors to make us work harder, but really it just humiliated the kids who just didn't understand the material. But Jackson never had to worry about that. His grades were exceptional, and always better than mine. Still, I didn't worry about him as a potential threat because I had trained with Dad, I was the future commander, and I knew how to play my part well.

Looking back, I was an idiot. I was arrogant and sure of things I knew next to nothing about. I thought that because I was trained with my future in mind, I would always be the best.

Coach addressed the class that day with four Operatives, all sent to help him begin our training. He sectioned us into four groups and we took turns fighting the Operatives in basic hand-to-hand combat. I remember being put in the same group as Jackson and barely watching when he took the mat. Maybe I was distracted by Gretchen, who had taken the mat beside ours, and I was worried. Or maybe I just didn't think he would show anything worth my attention. But then I heard a body hit the mat hard from in front of me, and I spun around to see Jackson had flipped the Op over and was preparing the final strike, when Coach called the fight. A hush moved over the room as all eyes focused in on Jackson. He was smart and athletic and fit, but still, he was from Landings, which meant we had overlooked him—all of us. I had always felt for Landings people, though that didn't change the fact that I still felt those of us from Process were more capable, more driven—better.

Jackson was the only student to win a fight that day. A Landings boy, the only one to win. No one could believe it, least of all me. As it happened, class ended before I had a chance to fight. I told myself I would have also won. Of course I would have won. I was Ari Alexander, after all.

Now, I feel sure that I would have lost and lost big. Because my training supported my belief that I was above everyone else—at least in terms of ability. Sure, Dad was hard. Sure, Dad told me over and over that I needed to be better. But he also taught me that because of who I was, with his help, I would get there. I was taught to think and act as though I knew nothing of being an Operative, but at the same time, I was also taught that I was already above average, already great.

Jackson's skill is self-imposed. He is good not because he was taught that he was great, but because he was taught— is taught—that he was nowhere near enough. And that difference is why I feel sure that if I'm going to survive here on Loge and stand a chance of getting back home, I need to think less like Ari and more like Jackson.

We enter the house and Jackson says he's going to grab something, for me to meet him out back.

I walk outside, taking in the flowers and the grass, the stone carvings that Vill must have made. The fence is high, and I'm unable to see over it. I wonder if anyone can hear us back here or if it's private.

I hear the back door close and turn around to see Jackson

coming toward me, a ball in his hand. "Can anyone hear me out here?" I whisper.

He laughs. "Zeus is the only one who cares to listen to what people are saying. Here," he says, motioning around to the other houses, "we have each other's backs. You're safe."

For some reason his words give me goose bumps. He had always said Logeans were kind beings, but I had no idea they were also so loyal to one other. It's a nice change from what we often see back home, where people argue over everything and anything. "Good." I start toward him, excitement in my voice, but I can't help it. "See, I know this is going to sound crazy, but I think Cybil was faking." Jackson turns his head just a touch in a way that says he definitely thinks I'm crazy and each word is only further proving his theory. I wave an annoyed hand at him. "Don't judge yet. You haven't heard me out. Listen. She smiled when they put her back into her bed. Just a twitch, but I saw it and she knew I saw it. She did it for me, to let me know."

"Ari, she was medicated. She likely—"

"No, trust me. I know Cybil. She's been trained for this sort of thing." I lower my voice still more and edge closer to him. "Lancaster said two Operatives were sent here. Maybe Cybil is one of them. Maybe she can help."

He shrugs. "It's possible."

"Maybe we can have Cybil fake an episode like the one you mentioned the night we tried the first plan. Zeus goes there and so do we. We apprehend a few of the guards on the way, then kill Zeus, and slip back out before anyone realizes what has happened."

"That won't work," Jackson says, tossing the ball from one hand to the other. "The Vortex is monitored. The moment we take out a guard, someone will know, and Zeus will be notified."

I sigh. "Then what? We have to think of something."

"We will," Jackson says.

"When?"

"Ari, we have one go at this. One shot. We mess that up and everything is ruined. We can't rush this, do you understand? We have to think it through. Make sure all our bases are covered."

I release a breath. "You're right. I just feel like we're speeding toward our doom, doing nothing."

"Everything we do has a purpose. Even this." He holds out the ball.

"Okay, fine, what's this about." I motion to the ball.

He tosses it again. "Today the RES would have worked on reflexes. I don't want you to get behind, so…"

"Okay, you're going to throw a ball and I have to catch it?"

"Something like that." He steps closer to me. "The ball is a distraction. I need you to focus on what I'm doing and what the ball is doing, using your reflexes to their max to maintain order with both. Make sense?"

"Not really," I say. "Wouldn't it be better if you just hit me and I have to block it or something?"

Jackson crosses his arms, a smirk on his face. "Let me get this straight. You want me to hit you?"

"Would it be better if I hit you?"

At this he breaks into hysterical laughter. "I'd like to see you try. Remember, Ms. Commander, I was never allowed to show my abilities back in Sydia. I'm faster than you and stronger than you. You can't hit me."

A smile stretches across my face just before I lunge for him.

Jackson jumps out of the way and wraps one of my arms behind my back. He leans close into my ear, his breath on my neck. "Tell me you've got more than that, Alexander." A tingly feeling spreads from my neck down my spine, settling over me, and I have to force myself to draw a breath so I can focus enough to separate myself from him.

I brush my hair out of my face and peer up at him. "How did you do that? I barely saw you move."

"Technique." He grins.

I roll my eyes, but can't help but smile back. It's nice to see him joking around, acting so normal.

"Well are you going to just stand there with that stupid smirk on your face or are you going to teach me these techniques?"

"I'll teach you," he says.

He tosses the ball around in his hands, his muscles flexing with each move, and then suddenly he chucks the ball into the air. I have no idea when I decided to move, but moments after the ball released from Jackson's hand I darted left, somehow knowing which way it would go. I grab the ball with one hand and toss it into the other, before throwing it back to Jackson with a nod. "Again." He bounces the ball on the ground, never letting his eyes leave mine and then fakes right before tossing it to his left. I lurch forward as the ball begins its decline to the ground and then dive forward, only to end up covered in dirt and grass, the ball a few feet away from me.

"You're faster than that." Jackson reaches out to help me stand. "You can't focus only on the ball. Remember, I'm the one deciding where the ball will go. It doesn't have a mind of its own. Sure, feeling the ball will help you, but that isn't enough. You need to anticipate my moves. Watch me, not the ball."

We go again and again, Jackson throwing the ball around and me catching it, until I'm moving almost as quickly as he releases the ball, guessing his moves as soon as he makes them. He dribbles to ball on the ground, night settling in overhead. "Now you're ready for tomorrow."

"What will they use tomorrow? A ball, like this?"

He tosses the ball to the other side of the yard and holds open the door for me. "Not exactly."

"Then what?"

"You'll see."

CHAPTER 11

That night after dinner, I sit out on the front porch by myself, just watching as the Logeans on our street go about their lives. Some sit on their porches like me, while others play some game in the street. I watch the game, curious how they keep track of who's winning because to me all it looks like is a bunch of people kicking and hitting a ball to each other, never letting it touch the ground. I'm trying so hard to figure out the game, that I don't notice Vill until he's sitting next to me. "Interested in playing?" he asks, then laughs at the look I give him in response. "Didn't think so."

"I just don't understand it. How do they keep score? I mean, what's the point? I can't even tell who is on what team."

Vill props his elbows on his knees and his chin in his hands. He looks like a child sometimes, and I find myself wishing I could ask him how old he is. "You're thinking about it all wrong. The game isn't meant as a competition between two groups, where one beats the other. They're supposed to work as a team, so if the ball comes to you and you let it fall, you're out. The goal is to keep it going, to work as though you are one. Understand?"

I turn back to the game, watching as the ball moves from person to person, never landing. They laugh and scream out as the ball almost drops and one of the boys has to dive to keep it from landing. "So it's not a game, really, then? It's more a way to work together?"

"It's how we are, Ari. Logeans are not one against all. We are all against one."

My eyes lift to his. "And who is the one?"

Immediately my thoughts drift to Zeus or even humans, and I'm surprised when Vill says, "It's whoever or whatever challenges us in that moment."

I smile. "You sound like Emmy."

He leans back in his chair with a laugh. "You're not the first to say that, I'm afraid."

"Really, why?"

He holds my gaze. "Emmy is my grandmother."

"Wow, I had no idea," I say, checking to see if there is any resemblance, but finding nothing. "I think a lot of her."

"And she you."

I stare up into the night sky at the two full moons that look down at us like glowing eyes. The rest of the sky is black except for the stars, and if it weren't for the second moon, it would look just like our night sky back home. Just thinking about home causes me to smile a little. I never imagined it would be possible to miss something so badly. And it's more than just the people. I miss the familiarity of everything—the clothes, the foods, even the auto-walks that ran from place to place. I miss waking up in my bed and knowing, for the most part, what the day would bring.

I used to get so annoyed at how rigid Dad was, how he ran his entire day by a schedule, but now I understand. He liked to know what to expect. And while I would never say that I'm as rigid and orderly as Dad, I now know that I don't like surprises or unknowns. Which is all the more reason why I can't wait to talk to him about Cybil.

Jackson sent Law a note just before dinner, but I haven't heard from him whether Law responded and it's getting late. I tell Vill goodnight and head in to go to bed. I slip inside and lie back on the bed, my mind a blur of thoughts and confusions.

Jackson comes inside and closes the door behind him. "Are you okay?"

"Yeah…just thinking."

Jackson flattens out on the bed beside me, his arms over his head. "What about?"

"Mainly, me. Everyone has so much faith in me. The leaders. Emmy. But what if I'm not that girl anymore? What if what made me so strong was the people around me and without them I'm lost? What if—?"

"Ari…" Jackson places his hand on mine and rubs small circles to try to calm me, but it's no use, the reservoir has opened and I have to gasp through the onset of sobs to try to breathe.

"I just—I can't—I'm not…"

"You are, Ari. You've just lost yourself a little, but we'll find her again. Don't worry. The Ari I lo—know is still in there."

My eyes snap to his at the slip and I wonder if he was about to say what I think he was about to say. Surely not, but I can't keep the warmth in my chest from spreading at the thought. The truth is, I'm not sure about Jackson—or at least the Jackson I felt I knew. But everything I have learned about the Jackson he is here is so much more than I could have ever guessed. From his care for his grandmother, to his fear of Zeus, everything about him feels so much more…real. And each day I find myself wanting to dive deeper into his world, to learn a little bit more about this Jackson, because if possible, I think I can see myself falling for him on a completely different level from what I felt for Jackson Locke.

I wipe my eyes with the heel of my hand and release a long yawn. I have no idea what time it is, but I'm exhausted in every way. Jackson notices the yawn and begins to sit up. "I'll just…" He motions to his bed on the floor. And I'm torn. I don't want to lay in this big bed alone, but I don't want to suggest that I'm ready for something I'm not. I'm still learning who Jackson is and though everything I've learned tells me I can trust him, I'm not ready to go there.

Jackson scoots to the edge of the bed, his back to me, and I have no idea why or what causes me to do it. Maybe it's the fact that he sees me as what I can be instead of the vague mess I feel like I've become. Maybe it's because he understands how much I miss my family. Or maybe it's just because I want a warm body beside me, but I reach over and tap his back without allowing myself to over think the consequences. "Do you think…I mean, would you mind if you laid beside me for awhile? Just until I fall asleep?"

His eyes slide over my face. "Whatever you need." He lies back down in the same place he was before and I shut off the lights before lying down beside him. We aren't overly close. No parts of my body are touching his, but still I feel him there, his warmth, his certainty. I close my eyes and breathe him in, feeling so unbelievably relaxed that it's all I can do not to reach out to take his hand.

He shifts beside me, and his leg grazes mine, sending a surge through me. I wonder if he can feel it there too or if he's already asleep and doesn't realize what he's done. I count my own breaths, trying to force my mind and heart to calm down enough to sleep. But I can't seem to settle down. It's too dark in the room to see anything clearly, so I chance a glance over at him to see if he's awake. His eyes shine back at me, and the moment is still, nothing present but us and our beating hearts. No complications or lies. No worry or threat. Just Jackson and me as we are today. My heart swells as I stare at him, and I wonder if this is what it's like to actually fall for someone. It's slow and steady, not rushed by fear or the threat of losing everything you love. No, it's just a girl and a boy, staring into each other's eyes, lost to anything but each other.

I don't know if I'm falling. But I do know that of all my moments with Jackson, this one is my favorite.

. . .

I wake hours later to find myself curled up in the nook of Jackson's body, his arm tucked tightly around me. For a moment I stay there, feeling his slow breath against my face as his chest rises and falls. I know it must be time for our call to Law and even though I hate to move, I wiggle out from Jackson, only to have him pull me closer and nuzzle into my hair. "Jackson," I say, tapping his chest.

"Hmm?" he asks, then he must realize how entangled we are because he jerks up, rubbing his eyes and stretching. "What time is it?"

"I don't know, but I thought it must be time to call Law, right?"

He stretches his arms out and stands, not at all addressing how we had slept. "You ready?"

A minute later, and we're back in Jackson's hidden office, staring at the screen while it tries to connect. On another monitor, Jackson is messaging Law to make sure he's still available. He sends the signal to the satellite to open the wormhole, which sends our message to Earth's satellite.

We wait. My eyes dart between screens, and then simultaneously Jackson has a message flash on his screen and my screen scrambles before Lawrence appears. I smile brightly when I see him and reach out to touch the screen, even though it isn't like I could actually feel him. It's still so overwhelming to see him after what feels like so long.

"Law?" I ask. "Is that really you?" The last time I saw him, he was different, distant.

He laughs. "Let me guess, they forced you to take some memory thing that washes away all reminders of humankind. I'll try to bring you up to speed. I'm Lawrence Cartier. One of your best friends. Generally awesome guy—wildly attractive, great personality, strong sense of humor."

"All right, all right," I say, waving my hands in the air. "I changed my mind. Put on Gretchen." We both break into laughter and it feels so good seeing him without everyone else around that I almost cry.

He leans in closer to the screen. "How are you?"

"I'm good. Well, as good as I can be. I miss you, all of you."

Law's gaze travels behind me and I turn to see Jackson watching us with a strange expression on his face.

"How is he treating you?"

"You mean your brother? Great. Jackson is great. And there are others here who are great. What about you, how is everyone there?"

Law tenses visibly and I start to question him when he says, "Things are changing, Ari. There's a lot going on. I'm not sure how safe this feed is to discuss it."

"Are you worried?" I ask.

Law hesitates, which is answer enough, so I dive into everything I know so far. What Emmy told me, my theories about Cybil, the humans, Zeus. I even tell him about Lydian torturing me about the entrance. I hear Jackson shift in his chair as I'm describing it, and I know I'm going to hear it later. Law listens quietly until I'm done and I expect him to give me immediate answers, when instead he looks behind him and then back at the screen. "We're going to run some analysis on this connection just to be safe. Can you call again tomorrow?

We'll know by then how safe it is to talk openly. I can't risk…
well, you understand." His expression, so tense, causes a shiver
to run down my spine.

"What's going on? Why do I feel like things are worse
than you're letting on?" Law scratches his chin and looks away.
That's when I realize he isn't alone. I try to spot someone else
from the view I have, but they must all be behind the screen
he's talking into. "Law, who's with you? Is it Dad? Can I talk
to him?"

He releases a long breath and looks past me, either to
Jackson or someone in the room with him, I'm not sure.
"Tomorrow. For now, try to stay safe." And then the screen
scrambles before returning to black.

CHAPTER 12

"Why didn't you tell me he was torturing you?" Jackson says, closing the door to our room, his tone so angry I'm worried any answer I give is only going to send him over the edge.

"You mean, like you told me he was torturing you? You think I don't know what all that blood means? I do."

He looks away. "That's different."

"Is it? Do you think I want him hurting you?"

"I can take it, Ari. I've dealt with Zeus my whole life. It's different for you. You don't know how far he'll go."

"I know that," I say. "But what am I supposed to do? I don't even know what he's asking me. Something about an entrance, but I don't know to what or where." I lay down on the bed, so exhausted, yet so rattled, my body is torn between passing out or going to work out.

Jackson lays beside me and pulls me into him. He kisses the top of my head and nuzzles into my neck. "We'll figure it out."

I let the sound of his breathing carry me to sleep, only instead of rest, I'm greeted with a new nightmare of places I've never visited and horrors I have yet to imagine. I have no idea what the nightmare is about or who it involves, but when morning wakes me, I'm covered in sweat, one thought on my mind. No one will be safe until Zeus is dead.

. . .

Too few hours later and I'm walking with Vill to see Emmy before my RES training. It's a beautiful day and I wonder if I'll ever get used to the lavender toned sky. We've yet to have rain, and I wonder if that has anything to do with the limited water on the planet. Maybe they've been in some constant drought. I'm not sure, but the more I learn about Loge, the more questions I have. I wish I could sit down with someone and just fire away—How do they travel through the trees to Earth? Do they travel from the trees here to the trees there or do they just close their eyes and somehow they're on Earth? I know that no one is traveling there now, but still, I'm curious how it works. And what about the rest of Loge? I know there are other cities with limited civilization like Triad, but how do you get to them—*can* you get to them?

And then there are the more pressing questions like how long do we have before Zeus attacks Earth, because he will. He said so himself. Yet beyond RES training, I've yet to see anything that resembles preparation for war, though maybe he would keep it hidden or maybe it's handled in another city.

"You know, your face crinkles up when you're deep in thought," Vill says from beside me. We decided to take the path that goes around the river instead of going by boat. Not that I mind the boats, but I would rather see as much of the city as possible and the path allows me more time to memorize where things are.

I sigh. "I know. My dad always said my expressions were my greatest fighting weakness. Oh and the thinking too much thing."

"Thought is never a weakness," Vill says in his usual philosophical way. "It's where you choose to focus your thoughts that becomes the weakness. I get the impression that you have questions. Why haven't you asked Jackson?"

I train my gaze on one of the factories as we near. They remind me of the apartment buildings in Landings—all metal and cold-looking. "He has a lot on his plate right now. I don't want to add to his stress, ya know?"

Vill watches me for a fleeting second. "I'm not sure I understand your relationship."

At that I laugh. "You and me both."

"You care for him, that is obvious, yet you push him away."

I don't want to talk about this, especially with Vill. And I have no idea what to say. Vill respects Jackson. It's obvious in the way he talks to him, and I find myself wishing I knew Jackson on that deeper level. "It's complicated," I finally say.

"Not really." Vill stops on the path so I'm forced to look up at him. "Nothing in life is actually complicated. Our minds are able to process complex things, therefore complications in life are due to our own failure to try to un-complicate them."

I shake my head. "Sorry, what? We're going to have to work on you speaking plainly to me if you want me to follow along."

Vill laughs out loud and starts back down the path.

"It's hard to feel sure that you know someone, only to learn that you never really knew him at all. I'm just more guarded this time. Jackson did more than lie to me, Vill. Sure, I would have helped him anyway. That much I'm sure of, because I never helped him because of him. I helped him out of desperation to save the people I loved. Still, we grew…close. And then all of it was swept away. He can't expect me just to forget."

"I don't think anyone is expecting you to forget. We just want you to see his reasons, to see him, for who he really is. He is nothing like Zeus."

"I know that."

"Do you?"

We head around to the back of the Panacea in silence to
where Emmy asked for me to meet her. She's already deep into
Juniper Gardens when we arrive and it takes several minutes
of searching for us to find her. When we do, she's kneeled on
the ground tending to a flowering bush that is half covered in
flowers and half dead.

"I have waited, children," she says as we approach, though
her back is to us. She continues to work through the bush,
bringing each leaf and flower back to life until the entire
bush is vibrant green with tiny pink flowers, and then brushes
off her pants as she stands. She then turns to Vill. "Are you
prepared?" Vill nods to her. "Very well. Ari, you understand
mind power?"

"Sorry, what?" I edge closer, glancing first at Emmy, then
at Vill.

Emmy stares beyond the fence to the decaying planet on
the other side. A shiver creeps down my spine as I follow her
gaze. How is it possible that something so beautiful can lead
to something so horrific? "I heal, therefore I am called healer,
so too the other healers, but…we are not alone in our ability.
Understand?"

I shake my head. "I'm sorry, no. You were born a healer,
right? That is why you are able to heal. You possess an ability
beyond that of other Logeans."

"But what if she does not," Vill says, breaking in. "What if
there is nothing in her genetic makeup that specifies her as a
healer?"

"I don't understand. Jackson said healers were rare in your
world. That they were born."

Emmy huffs at this. "He say what he told, child. Anyone
heal, just as anyone do anything. It our mind that wields power.
And that why you here with me today."

I glance back at Vill.

"Ari, we believe that anyone has the ability to not only heal, but to do virtually anything. It's about tapping into the true power of our minds and understanding that every molecule is directly impacted by every other molecule. Once you understand this, speed, action, even healing can be controlled by thought."

"But if that's true, then why would only specific people be able to heal?"

Emmy takes my hand in hers with a smile. "Your mind so thoughtful, child. Open it. See what there. We heal because we believe we can heal."

"So you're saying that anyone can heal? If that's true, why are there so few of you that do?"

"Because it's about belief," Vill says. "Watch. I'm not a healer. No one on Loge considers me a healer. If they did, I would be working at the Panacea instead of at the school. But yet…" He reaches out to the bush beside the one Emmy had been working on when we arrived. His fingertips glide over the brown leaves, and at first nothing happens, but then as his fingers float over the leaves again, they move and shift, uncurling from their half dead stupor. The leaves never return to green, as they did for Emmy, and the transformation is slower, but it's there. While Vill may not have healed the leaves that he touched, he did save them. They are no longer days or even minutes from death. They have hope.

"You just…" I point to the leaf and then turn to Emmy. "You said this was why I am here."

She smiles, her expression full of warmth. "Yes. I know what you must do. I know you need a means. I teach you to heal, so you use it to save us."

I glance from Emmy to Vill. "I don't understand how this can help. Maybe it can help me survive whatever he throws at me, but how will it"—I look around nervously and lower my voice—"help me kill him?"

Emmy smiles. "Healing about a lot more than plant life, child. It give you control of things around you. It a weapon. A weapon no one expect." "How?"

"The mind's a powerful thing, Ari," Vill says. "Imagine the possibilities if you were able to not only give life, but take it away ." My heart hits in my chest in rapid rhythm. If what they're saying is true, then I might stand a chance. I can kill Zeus and get our people home. "Vill, how long did it take you to get that far?"

He swallows hard as he looks up at me. "A while."

My heart sinks into my stomach. "I don't have a while. Zeus is planning his attack right now. I'll be lucky to survive the next few weeks."

Emmy cups my face with her hands. "You strong, child, remember that. Where you place your mind, greatness will follow. Have faith. We do."

CHAPTER 13

I make my way to the Vortex, my mind so distracted that I don't notice Madison calling my name until she is practically shouting in my face.

"Hey, are you all right?" she asks, running to catch up with me.

I shake my head to focus. "Yeah, just tired. How are you?"

"Good. You missed training yesterday. Were you sick?"

I open the door and hold it for Madison to go ahead of me. "No, Zeus requested to see me."

She gasps. "Zeus, wow. What did you do?"

I balance my gaze on her, wishing I could tell her the truth. So far, Madison is the only Ancient to talk to me beyond Vill and Jackson. I hate to lie to the only friend I have here so far, but telling her will do no good. "He wanted to make sure I was in RES training as he requested."

She looks puzzled. "Why wouldn't he just ask J.C.?"

I open my mouth to spit out another lie, when Jackson walks through the doors with Mackenzie. He holds the double doors for her, and she smirks my way. No doubt her attempt to remind me that I am nothing here. As though I need that reminder.

"Do you know Kenzie?" Madison asks in awe.

"Not really. I—"

"Let's go!" Jackson shouts at us from the door. "Training is about to begin, and you're out here gossiping. Focus!"

Madison rushes through the doors, her face bright red. I glare at him as I slip past him and into my spot in the lineup. That was so unnecessary. I stare forward, unwilling to look at him.

"Today, we will continue reflex training. Each of you will pair up and practice on each other. We will walk the floor and correct as needed. Get started!"

I glance around for Madison, who thankfully waves me over, because I have no idea what we're supposed to get started doing.

She walks to a table against the wall, grabs a pair of blindfolds, and passes one to me. "We take turns."

"Doing what?"

"One gets blindfolded and the other attacks. The goal is to use your other senses to defend yourself."

Mackenzie walks up before I can respond, clearly enjoying herself. "Is there a problem?"

"No, no problem." I slip the blindfold over my eyes, wishing I could do this without her or Jackson in the room.

"Well go ahead then," Mackenzie says.

Madison hesitates. I can hear her breathing grow heavy. She doesn't want to hit me, but even she must know that Mackenzie doesn't take well to weakness. I hear her draw in a long breath and then she throws punch after punch. I block the first few, but she's an Ancient and even though I'm trained, I'm new to this, and she's faster. Her fist connects with my jaw, and I stumble back, narrowly keeping myself from falling down. I shake my head to try to clear the pain and step back up. "Nice job," I say.

"I'm sorry. I didn't—"

"What are you apologizing for?" Jackson says. "Hit again."

Madison waits.

"I said, hit again."

I grit my teeth to keep myself from screaming at him. I know he's only doing his job, that he can't show favoritism, but this is absurd, as though he's intentionally being harder on me just to prove a point.

Madison pulls back to punch, but my anger has taken over now. I grab her fist and flip her around, shoving her hard to the cement ground, harder than I intended. She gets up slowly, and I realize in my haste, I might have actually hurt her. "I think it's my turn now," she says, and I can tell she wants them to leave as badly as I do.

I don't take off my blindfold. "Fine, switch, but I don't need to remove my blindfold. I can do this with my eyes closed, in the dark, with twice as many coming at me. You know that." I spit the words out at Jackson before I can stop myself.

Jackson steps up to me, rage radiating off him. "Your arrogance is going to get you killed."

I lift my head. "Don't belive me? Then you go against me."

A hush settles over the room, and I realize the others have stopped fighting, that they're all watching us. I hear Jackson removing his jacket. "As you wish."

I focus all my energy on Jackson, on his breathing, on the smell of his skin. I give everything I have over to my senses, listening, feeling, so when he throws the first punch, I'm ready. He hits again and again, me deflecting each hit or spiraling out of the way. We go on this way for a few minutes, my breathing growing heavier, then when I think he's about to stop and I momentarily drop my guard, he sweeps my feet out from under me and I fall hard, my head cracking against the cement. I try to get up, but the pain is overwhelming. I lay my head back down and give xylem a chance to heal me, though

I know it will take longer with me being only half Ancient. Several seconds pass before the pain begins to recede to a dull ache and I sit up, pulling the blindfold from my eyes.

Jackson regards me, then turns to address the group. "There is no room for arrogance here. Is that understood? Arrogance yields mistakes and mistakes will get you killed. See this as a lesson to you." And then he leaves the room without another word.

I follow after him, ignoring Madison's call for me to stop, and find him outside, pacing by the bridge.

"What was that?" I ask, seething.

"I could ask you the same thing."

"You just made me look like an idiot. Now they think I'm a weak fighter."

He shakes his head. "Now they think you're the toughest fighter in the room. How long do you think the rest of them would stand against me? Not a quarter of as long as you did. I just did you a favor."

"I don't need favors. I can fight. You know that. I don't need you using me to make a point to the others."

Some of the other Ancients have come outside now, and Jackson glances up, clearly aggravated. "This conversation is over."

I turn away from him and slam the door to the Vortex, not stopping until I'm down the spiral steps and pounding my way to Cybil's room. I'm tired of this, tired of Jackson's split personalties and Cybil pretending she's insane. I want the people I know to *act* like the people I know, so I can focus on what I have to do, because right now, I need solidity in my life. I need support.

I close the curtain and scrutinize the room, taking in every angle, and while I can't physically see any cameras, I know they're there. Zeus would never allow the humans to go unwatched. Which makes what I'm about to do all that much riskier.

I slide my chair roughly across the floor so I'm directly beside Cybil. Like before, she's sitting with her legs crossed on the bed, staring out into the room as though she's blind. I hesitate, and then sit down on the bed across from her. I mimic her pose so she's forced to look at me, though her eyes are not at all focused on me—or anything else.

I mouth the words, "Cybil. We are running out of time." And then wait for a reaction, which doesn't come. I scoot closer to her until our knees touch. "Cybil," I say out loud this time. "I know what to do, but I need your help." Still, nothing. I draw a long breath and crack each of my knuckles, one after another like I do when I'm in deep thought.

I have no choice. Zeus walks around as though everything is in perfect order. Emmy appears more nervous with each visit. And I'm no closer to learning anything from Lawrence. This has to start and it has to start today. I slip a tiny knife out from inside my pocket. The knives here have stone hilts and they don't retract the way ours do back home, but they're still sharp. It'll do what I need it to do today.

I take Cybil's hand and press the point into her skin, watching for a reaction. Nothing. *Blast, Cybil, don't make me do this!* "I know you're in there. I know it. I can feel your thoughts as though they are my own. You're too much of a soldier, Cybil, to go down like this. I know you. And I hope you'll forgive me for what I have to do." And then I stab the knife into her hand, cutting straight through so the knife tip comes out on the other side of her outstretched palm.

She screams and flails around, but she doesn't do what I thought she would do—ask me if I'm crazy or call me out or something that says she is still the Cybil I know. I start to worry that maybe she really is gone, when a set of guards storms into the room. They take in Cybil's hand, the knife still wedged through it, and then both are on me. The larger of the two—a male Logean who has at least a foot and a half on me and well over one hundred pounds—tosses me up against the wall. Jackson isn't here to order them to stop and something tells me they were waiting for this moment to prove to me that I'm no better than the rest of the humans here. The guard's hand wraps around my neck and he holds me against the wall in a death grip. I fight against him, kicking and clawing. My air supply is dwindling fast. Tiny stars flash across my vision. I put forth one more solid kick, but it's no use.

My body feels heavy, my head aches, and then I hear a voice beside the guard. "Drop her now, animal, or I click and your brains splatter across your buddy over there." The guard drops me to the ground and I suck in breath after breath, my eyes roaming up to see Cybil with a gun pointed at the guard who had me pinned to the wall, the other guard passed out on the floor.

I smile up at her despite the pain in my neck and head. "Nice to have you back."

CHAPTER 14

"You have to be the most stubborn person in existence. You realize that, right?" Cybil follows me out of her room so a pair of Logeans can clean up after the mess we made. Thankfully, both guards appear to be in working order now—or at least they will be. Cybil rubs the hand I stabbed, now tightly wrapped in those purification bandages the healers use. "Was it really necessary that you stab me? Couldn't you have just told me what you were going to do?"

I crack my neck, torn between excitement that I have Cybil here with me and frustration that she's reprimanding me. "What was I supposed to do? You weren't caving. Law is acting all weird. Zeus is asking about some entrance. I'm—"

Cybil abruptly grabs my arm, silencing me and I turn to see two guards marching down the hall, Zeus close behind.

"Ah," Zeus says, clasping his hands in front of him. "So wonderful to see that your health has improved, Cybil. You may join us in our discussion." He claps twice to call attention to himself. "Attention! Attention!" A few moments pass, and then one by one people step out of their rooms and into the spacious hallway.

They look uneasily at Zeus as though he could cause them to burst to flames just by looking at them. The fear he has evoked in these people is enough to make me wish I could take out Zeus, right here, right now. And then as soon as the thought completes in my mind, Zeus's head snaps toward me, his lips pinched together tightly. "Now, now," he says, his voice low but direct. Then he turns back to the crowd, though several of them continue to stare at me with curiosity.

"Today, you will all embark upon a new journey here in Triad. We have nursed you to health. Most are now strong and capable. It is time that you take your rightful posts in our societal system."

"What are you saying?" a man calls out, and it's as though his words slapped Zeus in the face.

Zeus lowers his head, his hands connected behind his back. "If there is one thing that I wish could be ingrained in your feeble minds, it is that of manners and respect." His head jerks and he blurts, "Respect: a feeling of deep admiration for someone or something." He eyes one of the guards and in a flash, the guard is in front of the man and then the man is limp on the ground.

"Make no mistake," Zeus says to the man cowering below him. "I will be respected."

He slowly walks down the center aisle, tsking and mumbling to himself as though he were two people trapped inside the same body.

He moves his hands back and forth, arguing with himself, and I realize that he is so much worse than I ever could have imagined. Strict, I can handle, even mean, I can handle, but outright crazy is another level of evil. Crazy does not understand limitations because a truly insane person who errs on the side of enjoying evil doings does not have a conscience to slow him or her down.

With Zeus, we have no idea what he will do next because he himself likely doesn't know. What will set him off, what will calm him down, could be the same thing depending upon the day and his mental stability at that moment. Watching him argue with himself in hushed tones, his back to us, is like watching a bomb ticking toward its explosion, knowing you have no way of predicting when it will go and having no way of stopping it.

I glance sideways at Cybil, who looks as freaked out by the whole thing as I do. Then my gaze travels to the rest of the humans. A few have backed into their rooms, trying to hide from the potential madness. Others stare, mouth gaped, eyes wide.

Zeus stops at the top of the steps, turns around, and then the doors behind him open and ten or more RESs march through the doors, down the steps, and face the humans. One pulls out a tablet and addresses the crowd. "If your name is called, step forward." He calls out names, one after another, men and women, then he says, "Cybil Lee," and I turn, wide-eyed to Cybil.

"What is this?" I whisper.

She hesitates, glancing at the men and women who have already taken their place with the RESs. "They're Operatives… all of them."

"Are you sure? How do you know?"

Her voice is rich with worry. "We keep tabs on all Ops, even the ones stationed outside of Sydia. Your dad made sure I knew them all by name. They're Operatives, Ari, I'm sure of it." Her name is called again, and she starts for the group, giving me one more nervous glance as she's sorted into a line.

The last name is called, and Zeus claps his hands again. "Congratulations, those of you called will join a specialized division of the RESs. The rest of you," he says, turning to face the other humans, who are all out of there rooms now—some men, some women, others children, "will depend upon your government to determine whether you live or whether you die."

"What?" I scream, stepping toward him.

Zeus's eyes flash. "I have issued an ultimatum to the leaders of Earth. We cannot maintain life on Loge. To show them how seriously we take this matter, we will publicly kill one human each day until they agree to coexist and agree to make me one of the world-wide leaders. The death will be broadcast randomly to all T-screens on Earth. They have until tomorrow morning to make their decision. That is all." He leaves before I can take another step forward. Fear and shock ground me to the spot. He can't do this. I won't let him do this.

The RES start for the doors, pushing the Operatives they selected to go with them. Cybil's eyes dart back to me and I shake my head, as completely in shock as she must be.

I need to call home. Now.

. . .

I go immediately back to my room, eager to tell Jackson what happened. I search the house, even going out back to the shower, but he's nowhere to be found. Then I slip into our room and find him asleep on the bed.

I close the door quietly behind me and edge near. He's lying on his stomach, sprawled out across most of the bed, one hand tucked under a pillow, the other extended as though to cover an invisible person beside him. His pants hang low on his hips and one of the legs is kicked up to his knee. His T-shirt is a wrinkled mess across his smooth, toned back, exposing a sliver of skin just above his pants. He looks so peaceful, more peaceful than I've ever seen him. I go over to the edge of the bed and sit down beside him, lost in the easy rhythm of his breathing. I should wake him—he would want me to wake him—but I don't.

My eyes trail over his messy hair, across his closed eyelids, to his parted lips and it's as though I'm back in Sydia, kissing him with recklessness in my room, wishing more than anything that all the problems would go away so I could just enjoy that moment—for at least a moment. Now…it all feels complicated. My heart, my body, every nerve and pulsing vein wants him.

I can't deny it, almost like an invisible force pulling me to him. And it's always been that way. The moment I learned Jackson was training to become an Operative, I became secretly fixated on him. I watched the way he moved and carried himself as though he were the one training to become the next commander, not me. But even though I feel this incredible force between us, I can't make my mind move past the lie. I've been here for weeks, learned more about him than I ever knew on Earth, but it still doesn't feel like much.

I know he cares about his grandmother above anyone else. I know he hates Zeus, yet on some level also respects him. I know he is a very skilled fighter and that he finds pride in knowing he's stronger and faster than most. I know his friends adore him, and I know they are very loyal to him. But beyond those things, what do I know? I used to think Jackson hid his true thoughts to be mysterious, but now I think he does it because he's seen and experienced things worse than most people and he's afraid to let on just how jacked up he might be inside.

The thought makes me so sad for him that it takes all of me not to lay down, wrap my arms around him, and promise to never let go. My eyes flash back up to make sure he's still soundly asleep, and then move down his broad shoulders, over the contours of his back, before finding the sliver of skin again. I've seen him with his shirt off, but this is different—we are different—and I shouldn't be looking at him this way, especially without him knowing, yet I can't take my eyes away.

I reach out to touch the exposed skin, but stop mid-motion as my gaze falls on a series of tiny markings on his back. They're darker than the rest of his golden skin, almost green, and so close together I wonder if they connect somewhere underneath his shirt. Unable to stop myself, I lean closer, so close my face is mere inches from him. I'm so distracted by the markings that I don't notice Jackson wake up right away, nor the strange stare he's giving me until it's too late. "Um, what are you doing?"

I jerk up. "I was—I mean I wasn't—it isn't what—" I clear my throat. "Nothing. I'm not doing anything. What about you? I mean, obviously you were sleeping but why in the middle of the day?"

He looks away at the question. "Oh, I just had a—wait, stop trying to change the subject. Why were you about to kiss my back?"

My face lights up with embarrassment. "That wasn't what I was doing. I was…"

He cocks an eyebrow at me and sits up. "You were…?"

I have no idea what to say. If I admit that I was looking at the markings, he's likely to get self-conscious, maybe even angry. But I don't want him to think I was being weird either. I decide on the truth. "You were sleeping when I came in, and I just…I wanted to watch you sleep. I'm sorry." His eyes find mine and the warmth I feel so often around him returns. He has a way of piercing me with his stare, as though he can see me more clearly than anyone else has dared.

"I'm sorry," I say again, looking away. I expect Jackson to question me more, when instead he changes the subject.

"I'm sorry about earlier."

For a moment I have no idea what he means, then I remember RES training. It feels like days ago after what I just witnessed. I waste no time, diving directly into what happened. I continue on until I've given him every detail that I can remember. When I'm done, I let my gaze settle on his. "We need to call Earth."

Jackson stands, looking uneasy. "I'll go send the message. It smells like Vill made dinner. Go grab something to eat and we'll wait for Law or your dad to respond." He starts for the door and I grab his arm.

"What do you think's going to happen? Will he really kill someone every day until they agree to coexistence? The Ancients here won't stand by and let this happen, will they?"

He sighs. "You don't understand, Ari. Most of them aren't fighters, they don't have it in them. Whether they agree with what he's doing or not doesn't matter. They don't have the will to stand up to him."

"Not yet."

I feel a plan developing in my mind even before I've thought through how impossible it will be to implement. Most here fear him. Emmy is all but begging me to help get everyone to Earth. The Ancients aren't loyal to Zeus, they're just too afraid of him to stand up.

Well, that's about to change. It's time the Ancients rebel, and I'm just the girl to ignite the rebellion.

CHAPTER 15

An hour later, and we're out on the porch, waiting to hear from Law or Dad. Jackson keeps going in to check, over and over again, but we've yet to receive a reply or even a hint that he received our request. My nerves are wound so tightly my foot refuses to stop tapping and I've cracked every knuckle I have at least three times. Someone is going to die tomorrow, and unless a miracle occurs, we're not going to be able to stop it.

I place my head in my hands and rub my forehead, wishing I could think of something to do.

"Tell me about Earth," Vill says from beside me. I know he's just trying to take my mind off of things, but for some reason I decide to play along.

"Were you not there often?"

Vill shakes his head. "Only at night for the Taking. I've only seen what you humans wear to sleep." He laughs loudly.

"What? Did your assigned human wear something strange?"

He grins wide, almost embarrassed. "Ah, I wouldn't call it odd. He just wore…very little. He was an older man and thankfully he was always fast asleep by the time I arrived. I

don't know that I could have handled it if he were awake."
He shudders, and we both break into laughter at the thought.
"Most of us have very little experience with humans, which is
why you're so interesting to us here. We received our assigned
human and were told to go Take. I remember being so afraid
the first time. I had never seen a human before and it isn't
like our parents could go with us. I released from my Taking
tree and just stood there, staring at the small house with my
assigned human inside. They'd prepped us here on what to
do during the Taking and why. Xylem is sort of a strange
thing. It learns, advances, it becomes what it needs to be. But
originally, we could not at all fight off the basic illnesses of
your world. We tried. Zeus said we would Take to train our
bodies how to cope in your world. He never believed that we
truly needed you. Of course he was wrong and lots of test
subjects died."

"Test subjects? Do you mean…"

He nods. "He would have certain Logeans stop Taking to
see what the reaction would be. First a day, then a week, then a
month, each time sending them to Earth to live to analyze how
they sustained. Most died."

I don't realize I'm gripping my chest until Vill motions to
my hand. "I'm sorry. I didn't mean to scare you."

"It's okay. I just…I don't know, it sounds so cruel. I mean,
I can't imagine anyone would volunteer for those spots. It's
awful. I don't see how you tolerate him."

I have no idea what Jackson's upbringing must have been
like, but talking to Vill makes me wonder how he endured.
Any fear and control Zeus has over the rest of Loge must be
nothing compared to what life has been like here for Jackson.
An overwhelming sense of sadness washes over me and for a
moment all I can think is, *No wonder he lied about being Zeus's
grandson.* Who would want to admit to that horror?

Jackson comes back onto the porch, his eyes locking on mine, and I know I must be exposing everything I'm thinking, hanging it on my shoulder for any and everyone to see, but I can't push it away. I have never in my life met anyone more unstable and frightening than Zeus, and now looking at Jackson, knowing what he must have suffered, I realize that I have never known anyone as strong as Jackson. He's so guarded that I forget the sacrifices he makes daily, many of which are for me. The calls home. Allowing me to live here instead of with the other humans. The constant questions that Zeus would never approve of him answering. How many times has he returned home from training with blood on his shirt, only for me to push him further and further? I draw a jagged breath as the emotions threaten to overcome me. And as though Jackson is reading every thought I'm having, he comes closer, leaning in so only I can hear him. "You all right?"

Vill glances from Jackson to me. "I'll just…go get a drink. You two talk."

I nod, fighting to keep my tears in check as I focus on Jackson. "I'm sorry if I've made things harder for you. I — I had no idea it was so bad."

He shrugs. "I'm conscious when I make my choices, Ari, and regardless of what you think, I'm not afraid of what he might do to me. He can try, but he will never break me."

The conviction in his voice is so strong that I reach out for his hand without realizing it, intertwining my fingers with his, our eyes holding.

"Ari…"

I shake my head just a touch. "Don't. Not now."

He pulls me closer still, and I lay my head on his shoulder, needing his comfort and warmth. His breath glides down my neck. I know his lips must be close, and I want more than anything for him to kiss me, to feel his full lips envelop mine so

I lose myself in him. He draws a breath and blows out slowly, sending a cool breeze over my skin. And I can't help it, all control is somehow lost in the back of my mind. I tilt my head toward him, knowing I'm pushing this further than I'm ready to go. He pulls away to look at me, his eyes searching mine for answers, permission, something, and then suddenly everything gets bad.

Vill rushes back outside. "Emmy called. It's Mami. You have to go. Now."

Jackson is off the porch in one leap, walking so fast he's almost running. It takes everything in me to keep up with him, my heart banging against my chest the entire way.

Something is wrong, way wrong. A flood of emotions pours off Jackson in waves, his every feeling exposed.

We race past Zeus's building and around to the back, where a tiny path leads up to a massive house on a hill. The house is the same wood as the rest of the homes in Triad, but this house is four or five times larger than any other I've seen and constructed with as much glass as wood. There are no lights on inside the house except for a tiny one in the top left corner.

"Get her out of here," Jackson yells, and Vill wraps his hand gently around my arm to stop me.

"You shouldn't be here, Ari. I'll take you back."

"What?" My chest pumps from adrenaline. "I'm not going anywhere. What's happened to Mami?"

While we've been talking, Jackson is already halfway to the house, and I shake free from Vill to try to catch up. I don't want him to have to face whatever is inside alone…even if every part of me is shaking from fear. What has Zeus done to Mami to cause Jackson to rush here so quickly? I am almost to Jackson, when he wheels around, his eyes raging. "Go back with Vill."

I shake my head. "No. I can help you. I can—"

"Aren't you listening? I don't need your help! I need you away from here." Suddenly something crashes from within the house and Jackson's face pales. I take a step forward, every nerve in my body telling me to get in there, to help, to do something other than stand here and listen while whatever horror happens inside that house. But Jackson throws his hands up, urging me to stop, his anger so visible it feels like a living thing. He rakes a hand through his hair, his chest pounding visibly through his shirt. His eyes flash to Vill. "Get her out of here. Right now. Get her out of my sight."

I cover my mouth with a shaking hand, fighting hard to hold my emotions in. "Jackson…"

"Don't you get that I don't want you to see this? I don't want you anywhere near this. Just go. Please. Go!"

Another crash echoes from the house and he whips around then back to me, and I step away, not wanting his concern for me to keep him from doing what he needs to do. "Go."

Jackson disappears inside the house, and Vill tugs on my arm for me to go with him. I don't want to leave. I want to sit on the ground and wait. I want to go in and help. I want to do something so badly that my body twitches with the impulse. But I force myself, for Jackson's sake, to head back to our house. We're silent the entire walk, my hands linked by my mouth, while my mind tries frantically to figure out what just happened.

"Vill…" I say finally as we reach the house. "What happened?"

"I can't, Ari," he says and I feel my own anger bubbling to the surface.

"Tell me what's going on. What happened to Mami? Is it Zeus? What did he do?" But he just looks away as though I hadn't spoken at all. "Vill?"

He presses his lips together and looks down. "This isn't my story to tell, Ari. He wouldn't want me to say anything. He's…"

"So we're supposed to just wait here, not knowing what has happened or what might happen to them while they're there? Do you hear how insane that sounds? They could use our help. You don't just stand around while your friends are in trouble!"

"Look," Vill says, "I know you're built to act first and think later, but that's not the right way to deal with things here. Especially not with Zeus. If we get too involved he'll just take it out on J.C. or worse, Mami. The best thing we can do is wait for him to get back."

Without anything else to do, I find myself out on the front porch, in the pitch-blackness, my legs tucked up tight to my chest as I wait for Jackson to return. Worried thoughts rummage through my mind, each more terrible than the last. I wish I were one of those people who could think positively in bad situations, but I'm not and never have been, and right now all I can see is the combination of anger and terror on Jackson's face when we heard the second crash.

I lay my head on my knees, growing so tired it's all I can do to keep my eyes open, and then before I know it something startles me awake. I clamber to standing, my mind fuzzy as I try to figure out how long I've been asleep.

And then I hear what must have woken me.

Shouts cry out from inside the house and I stumble forward, shaking the last of sleep from my mind and blinking hard to try to focus my vision. When I reach the common room, Jackson and Vill are arguing.

"Back off," Jackson says, pushing Vill back. "I don't need your opinion on this. You haven't seen what I've seen. You don't have to wonder if today is the day they tell you she's gone. I won't let him hurt her anymore."

That's when I notice the metal piece in Jackson's hand. A small knife with an ornate hilt, but the way Jackson grips it tells me the knife must be much more of a weapon than it seems. I edge closer, unsure of what to say or do.

"I know how you feel. She matters to me too, but this isn't the answer. You're just going to get yourself killed. Besides, do you really think this is what Mami wants?"

Jackson shrugs the words away uncomfortably. "She doesn't know what she wants. She's willing to stay beside him out of loyalty. There is no reason to stay loyal to Zeus."

Vill flinches at Jackson's words, which just causes Jackson to shout louder, and then I can see it—see him slowly losing all control and sanity. He grips his head, the knife still in his hand. And in that second Vill storms him. But he has nothing on Jackson, who spins out of the contact and pulls the blade defensively.

"Don't!" I shout. And that's when Jackson's eyes land on me, wild and filled with so much hurt that it feels like someone punched me in the chest. He raises his hands in a helpless surrender and drops the knife to the ground, only to start trashing the room, breaking chairs and tables and smashing anything and everything he can find to throw.

Unable to watch any longer, I rush toward him and duck just as one of Vill's carvings comes hurling past my head. I grip Jackson's left hand hard and position myself in front of him, forcing his head to straighten with my other hand. Vill yells for me to get out of the way, and I can tell by his tone he's worried Jackson may accidentally hurt me.

"Breathe. Just breathe," I say to him, trying to hold his gaze on mine. "It's not your fault."

He stammers, his eyes everywhere, and then they finally meet mine…and my heart breaks into a thousand tiny pieces. He looks like a little boy, lost and afraid. "It's okay. Everything's okay," I say. Jackson, losing the fight in him, collapses to his knees, burying his head in my stomach. His body wrenches and

I know it's taking all his strength not to cry. I wrap my arms around him and say soothing things over and over until his breathing calms and the tension in his body relaxes. My mind reels with worried thoughts. What happened back there to cause Jackson to react like this? Is Mami okay? Is she alive?

"Come on, let's get you to bed." I eye Vill to help me, and that's when I notice the blood all over Jackson's hands and arms. "Is that his or...?" I whisper to Vill, petrified that he's about to tell me Mami didn't survive.

"His from all of this." Vill motions around the room, which is completely destroyed in every way.

"Does this happen a lot?"

"It's the first time he's lost it this bad."

I nod, not wanting to talk about Jackson anymore as though he isn't here, listening. Vill gets him to bed, while I wet a cloth to clean him up. Finally after several trips back and forth to the bathroom, we have his hands and arms clean and the cuts treated with some herbal ointment.

I close the door behind me, and whisper to Vill, "Can you talk for a second?"

He shrugs, but I can tell he's hesitant.

"Is Mami okay?" I ask, eager to know how she's doing, but also wanting to know how to handle Jackson if he starts talking about her.

Vill releases a long breath, and I can tell he's exhausted in every way. "She was very bruised when he got to her. She wouldn't tell him exactly what happened, though it sounds pretty obvious."

My eyes find the ground as I picture a fragile, bruised Mami. How could Zeus hurt her like this? Does he care for no one? "I wish I could have helped."

He shakes his head and starts for his room. "Jackson wouldn't want anyone else around."

"But he would have let you go."

"That's different. Mami is Emmy's sister, so she counts on me to help when I can. Plus, I've been around this for a long time. Jackson doesn't have to hide it from me." He yawns wide. "Let me know if you need help with him."

He closes his door and I'm left alone in the hallway with my thoughts. So Jackson and Vill are related. That makes sense. They've always seemed closer than friends, which explains why Vill was on me to understand what Jackson's life has been like here. He knows more than anyone else what Jackson has to deal with because he has seen it first hand.

I slip back into Jackson and my room, my stomach in knots.

I sit down beside him on the bed, brushing his hair from his face. He looks so young, so vulnerable, so absolutely wrecked. And then as though I'd spoken the words aloud, his eyes ease open and he whispers in a sleep fogged voice, "I'm sorry you had to see me like that. I shouldn't have..." He trails off, his eyes closing again. He's silent for several moments and I start to rise, sure that he's fallen asleep, when he reaches out for my hand. "Don't go. Just...can you lay with me?" I lie down beside him, staring at the ceiling, and wishing more than anything I could ask the questions running through my mind.

"He locked her in a room in the attic," Jackson says into the darkness. "By force. Like she was nothing, like he had never once cared for her. And what's worse, he makes her think she deserves it."

"I'm so sorry." I pause. "Why do you think she allows it?" I ask, hopeful that I don't sound insensitive.

Jackson adjusts on the bed, stretching his legs out and tucking his arms behind his head. "Fear. Hope. I'm not sure. I know she still sees the old Zeus in him, but I'm starting to wonder if that Zeus really ever existed or if this Zeus was always there, layers deep below the one we loved."

I clear my throat. "Do you think…it has to do with him losing your dad?" I cut my eyes toward him. I know next to nothing about his father and don't want to risk upsetting him more, but sometimes major events—like death—can change a person. Maybe that's what happened to Zeus. Or maybe he's just straight crazy and there is no logical explanation.

"No. Well, maybe. I didn't know him then so I can't say how that impacted him. All I know is that he wasn't this way when I was young and my dad died before I was born. I really think it's fear. I think he's afraid to trust humans and he lets his fear eat at him, change him. I just wish I could protect Mami. Every time I go there, my breath catches just before I see her, like any day she could be gone."

I close my eyes at the pain in his voice and without thinking reach over and link my fingers through his. "What set him off? I mean, was there something or did he just go crazy?"

Jackson adjusts again, this time obviously buying time. "It was…you."

I jerk up in bed and peer down at him. "What? What do you mean it was me?"

"She asked to see you. He refused. An argument ensued, and then as usual, he pushed her until she agreed to submit. She even apologized to me for asking to see you. Can you believe that? Said she should have known better." Anger and resentment swirl from his mind into mine and for a moment I get a taste of the Zeus Jackson sees—selfish, controlling, irrational, everything Jackson hates and everything he fights to avoid becoming.

"Why would he keep her from seeing me?" I whisper, though the real question I should be asking is, why did she want to see me? Somehow I feel certain she never shared that with Jackson. This feels more…private, like my meetings with Emmy, and perhaps Emmy has spoken with her about those meetings. They are sisters after all.

"Honestly? I don't know." He sighs heavily, and with that, silence overcomes us. I lie back down, my mind filled with worry. Zeus refuses to allow Mami to see me. Why? What does she know that he wants to keep from me or what might I know that he wants kept secret from her? Surely nothing, but then... Emmy claims I'm the one who will get us back to Earth.

I continue to work through all the possible reasons, and before long I hear the soft release of Jackson's breathing beside me. He's asleep, but I'm left wide awake, one thought on my mind, recurring over and over, building on itself with such passion that I feel as though my mind could explode from the madness at any moment.

I hate Zeus. I hate him with a deep, full longing that I have never felt for another person or thing in my life. I hate the way he walks, the way he talks. I hate the way he looks down upon you as though he knows so much more than you, more than you could ever know. But mostly...I hate that he has issued fear in Jackson, someone I thought was fearless.

I need to know more about Zeus, specifically more from the people who know him the most, and only one person can give me the answers I need.

It's time I meet Mami.

CHAPTER 16

I hear a knock on the door some hours later and slip from the bed to find Vill outside the door. "Someone has messaged you."

I follow him down to Jackson's office and he closes the door to give me privacy. The screen is already lit, the same formal group as the first call conjured together, though this time their faces show even more worry than before.

"Thank you for meeting with us," Kelvin Lancaster says, again at the head of the table. "We understand there have been some recent developments you would like to discuss."

I draw a deep breath, and launch into everything I know. Cybil. Emmy. What she has asked me to do. What Zeus has done with the Operatives, and finally I end with his threat to kill one human publicly until the leaders agree to coexist. "Is it true that he issued an ultimatum yesterday?"

Kelvin sits back in his chair. "It is. But we refuse to succumb to threats. As you know, we are prepared to offer a home to any on Loge who wish to come here. With the exception to Zeus himself. He is too dangerous to allow within our world. Which is why your mission is more important now than ever.

The sooner Zeus is dead, the sooner we can get everyone safely back to Earth."

"How am I supposed to do that, though? He's always guarded. He seems to know what is happening moments before it happens. He has a paranoia to him that is unlike anything I have ever witnessed."

"You will need a diversion," Dad says from the opposite side of the table. "From what you have told us, Ari, the people there are afraid of him. Use that fear."

I nod. "I think you're right. I think the only chance I have is to start a rebellion. We will have to put all plans in place so the night we move everyone to Earth, is the night I kill him."

Conversations start up around the table, some full of energy, others unsure. I wait for them to settle down and then direct my gaze at Kelvin. "I need assurance that you will do as you say. You will allow all Ancients and humans here to safely return to Earth. I will keep my end of this arrangment, but I need a guarantee that you will keep yours."

Kelvin laces his fingers together. "You have my word."

I notice Law tense beside him, almost imperceptibly, his eyes planted on the table in front of him. "Law?" I ask, and his head snaps up, his expression blank.

"Yes?"

Kelvin interrupts. "You may address President Cartier as such or as Mr. President during these calls."

"What? I thought you were the acting president."

"I am only the interium president. The true President of the United States is Lawrence Cartier."

I feel my insides swirl with sickness. Something isn't right here. "Law—Mr. President?" I ask, correcting myself before Kelvin gets angry and cuts the connection.

Lawrence trains his eyes on me, something empty inside them, so different than the Lawrence he was when we talked alone. I glance from Lawrence to Kelvin, wondering if Kelvin is the reason for the change. "You have a mission now, Ari," he says. "We expect you have work to do."

"But what about the humans? What about the daily killings?"

"We will handle that on our end. You need only focus on the task at hand. Start the rebellion. You have one week."

My eyes slip to my dad, and I see him mouthing something and then placing his chin in his hand, three fingers cradling his jaw. Three. What? I start to ask, when he shakes his head, and then the screen cuts out.

I sit there for at least an hour, staring at the screen, trying to reason what just happened. Something is wrong with Lawrence. It's like Kelvin has a finger on his pulse. And Dad doesn't seem to trust the others, I can tell by the way he remains quiet while they talk. That isn't Dad. What has happened back on Earth?

I pull myself from the chair and start back down the hall to Jackson and my room, but then decide better of it. The sun is beginning to rise, the first signs of day slipping through the windows in slivers of white. It's nearly morning and Zeus plans to kill one of our people today. I have to do something. I need to question Mami before everything gets out of control. And before Zeus ends up killing her.

• • •

"Hello, child," Emmy says as I approach her in the garden. She's on her knees, tending to a patch of grass that has turned yellow and brown.

"Emmy, that can't be good for your knees. Let me help." I reach my hand out, but she's already standing, a curious expression on her face.

"There's been a change," she says, eyeing me. "Your color is dark."

"I need you to teach me, Emmy." I drop down onto the ground beside the patch, my resolve in place. "Help me learn how to heal."

She kneels down beside me and places my hands over a patch of grass. "Feel it child. The individual. Each blade. Feel it."

I close my eyes and focus on the grass, on each blade as she says, and suddenly my palms begin to prickle. My eyes snap open to the grassy patch, but nothing has happened. "Why isn't it working?" I say, frustrated.

"Breathe. Focus." She places my hands back over the patch. "Try again."

I eye each blade as an individual being, with life within it, needing my life to rekindle it, just as Emmy said. My palm prickles again as the energy transfers from me into the grass. I keep my eyes closed, my mind clear of anything but the blades. I feel as though my energy is separating from my body, becoming a tangible thing that I can mold at my will. I open my eyes and smile up at Emmy. The blades aren't green, as they would be for Emmy, but they're no longer brown.

"Again," Emmy says.

I tune out everything but what I'm doing, and after several minutes of working, I've only healed an inch or two of the patch.

"Good try, child."

I sit back on my heels. "I thought I would be able to do it. " I rest my hand a few inches above the patch and concentrate with everything I have on turning the patch green. They remain the same yellow as before.

"You think too much."

"Yeah…I'm hearing that a lot lately."

"So clear your mind," Emmy says, pressing her hand over mine and within seconds the patch is fully green and alive.

I stare out past the wall of flowers to the dying Loge beyond, wondering how I ended up here. Just a few months ago my life was very normal. And now… "I want to see Mami," I say, unwilling to let myself focus on things I can't change.

She smiles. "I thought you might." And then before I can say another word, I hear someone walk up behind us and a meek voice say, "Hello, Ari."

"Mami?"

She smiles, and instantly I see where Jackson got his good looks. Her hair is vibrant white and so shiny she looks like she has stepped out of a fantasy world. She has it loose so it flows around her as she walks, and I find myself staring as though I'm watching something magical. Her eyes are the same green-blue of all the other Ancients—like mine—and against her light golden skin she looks much younger than what I know her actual age must be. In the moment, I'm torn between searching her face and arms for hints of the fight from last night and wanting to bow my head to her. Somehow, unlike everyone else I've met on Loge, she has a quality about her that suggests greatness or pureness or perhaps it's just that I know how much Jackson cares for her.

She stops a few feet from Emmy and me, and I know she is taking a great risk coming to see me like this. Surely Zeus doesn't know and wouldn't approve. "You are right, on both accounts. Though, regardless of what my grandson says, I do have a mind and choose to think on my own. There is just a great difference between acting out our thoughts and preserving them for quieter times. Do you understand what I mean?"

I lower my head a bit in embarrassment. "I do, though if I'm honest I have to admit that I'm not very good at that. Preserving my thoughts. I tend to show them fully the moment I think them."

"I see," she says, her eyes lit with humor. "I can see why Jackson is drawn to you. You are openly honest, even with those you barely know. It is an admirable trait. One I am sure you realize few possess." Her gaze pierces through me and I wonder if she is referring to Jackson hiding who he truly was or if she is simply stating the obvious—that few reveal themselves as openly as me, something I've been told since I was a little girl. My mom would laugh and say that my face was a picture to the depth of my soul. I always knew she appreciated this about me, maybe because she herself was that way when she was younger.

Dad, on the other hand, fought me continuously on the trait, reprimanding me for using facial expressions at all during training. "Your face can be a weapon for or against you," he would say. But what he never understood was that I prefer to be open, even if that makes me weak.

"You have questions for me. Come, let us discuss." Mami walks past me to a wooden bench further down into the garden. The path is more open here, and the flowers and trees larger and more enclosed, making it difficult to see the decrepit world beyond Triad. From this vantage point, you can almost forget that there is a dying planet, and instead all the beauty and smells of the garden overpower you.

Mami sits on the bench and pats the space beside her for me to sit as well. I take the seat reluctantly, not because I don't trust her, but because I'm unsure of where to take the conversation and I'm afraid of revealing something that perhaps I shouldn't know or asking a question that may make things even harder for her. I look away at the garden, trying hard to come up with something to say and feeling more and more uncomfortable by the second, when she takes my hand in hers, like Emmy does so often, surprising me. I turn to face her and instantly feel a pang in my chest for my mother. She looks at me like my mother looks at me—with care and understanding, as though nothing I could say would surprise or anger her. As though she is here just to make me feel more at ease. It's overwhelming and I have to look away before I start rambling on about all the things here that scare me, including Zeus.

"Why do you and Emmy sound so different? You were raised by the same parents, right?"

She laughs, the sound so full of life that I can't understand how Zeus—or anyone for that matter—could ever be mean to her. She's so…pure. "Do you have siblings, Ari?"

I shake my head. "No. My mother wasn't able to have another child after me. She calls me her little miracle." I feel my cheeks flush. I have no idea why I just admitted that to her.

"I see," she says, thoughtful. "Most children develop in different ways. Emmy chose to not speak for much of her childhood and then suddenly once she did, her language was clipped, hard to understand. My parents worked with her for years, but she chose to never fully develop her language skills. Many felt she was…challenged. But I'm sure you realize that Emmy is very bright. She never learned to speak correctly out of choice. Choice, after all, is a powerful thing. Which brings us to the true questions on your mind."

I look away, torn between the most pressing question and the most obvious. I go with the most obvious. "Jackson said you wanted to see me. Why? And why did Zeus refuse?"

She is thoughtful for a long time before answering. "I believe you possess a strong spirit. And I believe you want to protect not only your kind, but mine. I want to help you."

"So Zeus found out about it?"

At this she grins. She's a lot like Emmy, I realize. "You will learn one day, dear child, that there are many secrets to the female mind. Learning to hide them is part of our strength. Now, will you allow me to help you?"

I nod and she shakes the hand she's still holding, clasping her other hand on top. "Remember your strength today, Ari. You will need it. I will be as forthcoming as I am able and still protect you. Knowledge is a tool and too much can create enemies. My wish is to help you, so please trust that anything I refrain from saying is for your protection, not mine."

"My protection? I think I would rather know everything."

"A statement of the weak. We must prepare you to receive the information first, else your reflex to respond will overcome your good doing."

I try to let what she's saying absorb. "Mami, is he planning to kill all the humans here—Operatives as well as the other humans?"

"Yes."

I feel my pulse quicken. "Do you know when?"

"The Operatives will be used as shields when he attacks your planet. They will die by your soldiers' hands at Zeus's doing. The other humans will be killed daily, as you know. He claims this is unless your leaders agree to coexist, but truly that is just a diversion. He plans to attack regardless of what they agree to. He plans to take over Earth."

I gasp. "Take over? So there's nothing we can do? No agreement that can be made?"

"I'm afraid the time for compromise and discussion is over. I believe you have been tasked with a mission here?" She studies me, and I realize she knows I'm supposed to kill Zeus.

"I have."

"Then let me leave you. Time is not our friend, child, and you have work to do."

I leave the Juniper Gardens and walk around the river, to find a crowd forming at the bridge over Gaia Road. I slip through the group to the front, eager to see what's happening, and stop cold, my heart suddenly in my throat. A woman is standing on the railing of the bridge, her feet barely clinging to the wood. Tears stream down her eyes. She's visibly shaking. But none of that is what has me racing through the crowd, pushing men and women aside, my voice stuck in my throat, desperate to let out a cry for help. A noose surrounds her neck like a necklace, the end tied to the bridge's railing. I finally manage to scream, as a guard pushes her off the bridge, her body swinging out and then falling toward the water below.

"No!" I scream as I jump into the river. The water rushes up to my chest, colder than when I fell in from the boat. It feels like weeks since that happened, years. I scramble through the water, trying to swim, but fear has locked down my limbs. I see the woman's body swinging helplessly a few inches above the water's surface, and I have to get to her, I have to save her. I knew Zeus planned to kill a human, but somehow I thought it was only a threat, a cheap trick to get Earth's leaders to listen. How could I be so stupid? I finally reach the woman and try to lift her up, give her a chance to breathe, but she's heavier than me and I can't hold her, I can't hold her. I grunt from the effort, my arms burning, as I scream over and over for someone to help me, to please help me. The crowd begins to disperse, no one willing to go against Zeus. I feel a cry burst from my lips as her legs stop thrashing, the warmth in her body replaced with cold.

"No, no, no. Please, no. Please no."

An arm wraps my waist and pulls me back. "Shhh."

"No, let me go, let me go." I fight and kick against Jackson, who is waist deep in the water, angry that he let this happen, angry that I wasn't here to stop it.

I suck in a breath and wheel around in the water. "How could you?" I sob.

Jackson looks as miserable as I feel. "I didn't know he was about to do it. I was at the Vortex. I didn't know, Ari. You have to believe me. I would never have just stood there while this happened. I wouldn't."

I bury my head in his chest and cry so hard my body aches

from the effort. Jackson helps me from the water, both of us at a loss for words.

Kelvin said they would handle it. He said they would help.

I glance up to Zeus's building, rage building inside me, and see him standing clearly at his office window, watching, no doubt with pleasure, at his latest evil deed .

· · ·

I arrive at the Vortex fifteen minutes later to find Cybil and the other Operatives out in the field, the RESs running them through various conditioning exercises. I wonder if they know what just happened. Surely they do. Cybil looks concerned when she sees me, nodding toward the Vortex. I pick up speed, suddenly worried something else horrible has happened.

I race down the spiral stairs to where I know the other humans are, careless to the fact that I'm now late for my own RES training, but I will take whatever punishment they throw at me. I burst through the doors and stop at the top of the steps that lead down to their curtained rooms. The area is silent. Eerily silent.

I slow my pace, my eyes peeled. Even the acclimated rooms have the curtains closed today. I open the first curtain and peer inside, only to stumble back, my hands over my mouth. A boy lay in the bed, his mouth covered, his arms and legs restrained to the bed. His eyes widen when he sees me and he begins to shake all over.

"It's okay," I say, as I enter the room. "I'm not going to hurt you." I pull the bandaging from his mouth and he sucks in a breath before starting to cry. He can't be more than twelve years old. What reason could Zeus have possibly had to do this to him? Unless he did this to all the humans to guarantee they wouldn't interfere with his killing.

I quickly release the boy's arms and legs from their restraints and check the next room, to find a woman in the same condition, her mouth covered, her arms and legs tied up. Anger slices through me so quickly I feel like I might lose control. "What happened to you?" I ask, and the lady shrinks back as though I might hurt her. "I'm sorry. I didn't mean to startle you. What happened to everyone?"

She shakes her head. "I don't know. When I woke up this morning, I was like this."

I nod, fury wrecking me inside and out. Zeus must have ordered them to be restrained during their sleep to prevent any issues with his killing.

"Help me untie the others," I say to her and then the boy. We go from room to room, freeing all the humans. Zeus must see what I'm doing, but he never sends in anyone to stop me. Something tells me he enjoys watching me do this, enjoys knowing I'm cleaning up his mess. The realization of just how cruel Zeus has become sends a wave through me and suddenly I'm back through the doors of the Vortex, racing toward Zeus's building.

It feels as though my blood is on fire, rippling through my veins in succession, burning me up inside and then repeating the pain over and over. I slip into his building, ignoring everything around me, afraid that if I stop for a moment and allow myself to actually think, that my fear will overcome my determination.

I reach his office, expecting to burst in, only to have Zeus himself open the door for me and stand to the side while I rush in . He has a smirk on his face that tells me he knows exactly why I am there.

"You can't do this," I say, my adrenaline causing me to sound almost frantic. I need to calm down. I need to regain control of this situation.

I draw a long, steadying breath and spin around to face Zeus, each second helping me regain my composure. "Are you going to speak or continue to stare?" His jaw tightens, and once again I'm glad that I'm not afraid to die.

Zeus walks over to the wall of windows behind his desk, peering out as though he sees something intriguing. "As usual, your attitude is less than impressive. Impressive: evoking admiration through size, quality, or skill. But we shall fix that soon enough. For your comment, I can and shall. Instead of coming here to question me, you should be asking yourself why your worldwide leaders allowed this. I warned them. They chose not to respond."

I realize coming there, expecting to convince him of anything, was stupid and pointless. I try a different approach. "The humans could be useful to you. You don't have to kill them."

He releases a hollow breath that must be his version of a laugh. "Your mind is so absurd. It is difficult to take seriously."

"Excuse me?" I take a step forward and he turns, the same grin I've grown to hate on his face. The grin that says he is already so far ahead in the conversation that I may never catch up.

Zeus walks over slowly, his hands clasped behind his back. "Your wild nature is becoming a problem, as I am certain you are well aware. So tell me, how would your father handle an Operative who spoke to him with as much disrespect as you issue to me?"

I steel myself to block my thoughts and emotions from Zeus, knowing that if I keep my mind open it will just confirm what he is pressing me to say—that Dad would never tolerate my behavior. My mind flashes to my training with Dad, and I feel a tiny slip in my resolve. I never imagined in my life that I would miss those grueling mornings when I wondered if my dad loved me at all. I remember trying so hard at such a young age, only to have him yell at me again and again to try harder, that I wasn't good enough, that I was embarrassing him. Even thinking about it now, I feel a sharp pang in my chest.

But still, I would give anything to go back there now. I would do exactly what he asked and stand tall and fight hard. Because now I know, he was never training me for a fight. He was training me to survive if he were not around. Little did I know how quickly I would need those skills or how quickly they would slip when I needed them to surface the most. I think to Dad's face at the last call, to the three fingers he used to signal something to me that I've yet to figure out.

Zeus gives me a knowing look, and I'm afraid I've let my mind slip and he now knows about the calls home, but instead he continues. "Death would be an easier punishment for one of your father's soldiers. Am I correct? He was, after all, a hard man, the sort who enjoys breaking his men before he builds them back up. I imagine he—"

"That's enough. You don't know him, so don't speak as though you do. You know nothing about him and nothing about me," I spit out, my fists clenched so tightly that my nails are near drawing blood.

"Don't I?" He walks around me, rocking a bit as though he is completely at leisure. He leans into my ear as he passes behind me. "I know that he is a feeble man who pretended to be strong."

Even as my body moves, I recognize my mistake, almost as though I am watching from above, calling out to myself to stop, to calm down, to not fall into his trap. But he's right; I am wild—my mind, my control—and that sort of untamed passion can only be contained for so long.

I reach around, grabbing him behind the neck and shoving him toward his desk with such speed and force that he is unable to fight back. I don't think as I move, instead allowing my senses to overcome logic, telling my muscles what I need them to do. I shove his head onto the polished wood and pull the knife Jackson had last night from my pocket, glad that I decided on a whim to keep it. Enough planning, I'm ready to do this. Right now. The blade presses into his neck, and then I'm hit hard from the side by a body two or three times my size. The guard clamps my hands down above my head and sits on my legs so I'm unable to move, though I continue to push against him, fighting and kicking until he punches me hard in the face, silencing me with one blow.

When I wake, I'm back in the blue room, alone and unsure if I'm in a dream or if my head is still foggy from the hit. I reach up to my face and feel a large lump on the side of my left eye that seems to be swelling more by the second. I push myself off the ground to standing and find that I'm already surrounded by the blue lights, only this time they are further away from me. Lydian waits behind the glass across from me, and I can tell by her expression that she doesn't want to do whatever she has been ordered to do to me.

Try to stay calm. Lydian's voice rings through my ears as soft as a whisper, though as clear as the glass she waits behind. Her tone is different today, though. A warning. I find her eyes, and seeing the seriousness in them know whatever I'm about to face is going to push me in ways I never imagined. She closes her eyes and Jackson walks into the room, slipping inside the blue lights as though they are not there at all. I realize almost instantly that he is part of the test, but I can't keep my heart from picking up at the look on his face. He doesn't see me — or at least he doesn't see me as who I am. I've never seen this side of Jackson from this vantage point. His expression is fierce, his body tense and prepped for an attack.

"Where is the entrance?" he asks.

"Don't do this," I start to say to him, but before the words can fully leave my lips he's preparing to fight me. He widens his stance and focuses on me, hatred etched into his face. I wait for him to make the first move, and after several long seconds, I wonder if perhaps I have it all wrong. But then he pulls out the knife that I took from him from his own pocket.

He smiles wickedly at it, and then he's in front of me, slicing the blade over my arm and cheek, nearly clearing my chest before I've righted myself enough to respond. Instantly, a surge of pain radiates from the two wounds and I have to remind myself that this is only happening in my mind. I jump back just as Jackson swipes his blade again, narrowly missing my other arm, and continue to step backward until I hear a *zzz* and feel a shock against my back. I spin around to see the blue bars flashing, the lights so bright that for a moment I'm blinded.

And that's when Jackson grabs me from behind and tucks the knife below my chin, pressing into the delicate skin there. I try to pull free but with each tiny move, the blade cuts deeper into my skin until I cry out. "Okay, okay." I arch my neck back in hopes of relieving the pressure of the blade against my skin, only to have Jackson press it still closer.

My eyes scan frantically for Lydian, but it's Zeus I find behind the glass. He presses his palms into the table in front of him and stares at me with a grin that says this is only the beginning of what he has in store for me.

I force myself despite my fear to smile, knowing Zeus would never expect it, and then lean into the knife until I feel it slice across my throat, sending a stream of blood down my neck and soaking my shirt. As if in slow motion, Jackson drops my body to the ground, the pool of blood surrounding my face, my hands, my everything. And while I know that I am not dying—after all I have felt what it feels like to almost die—this is close, so close that for a moment I fear that I've made too bold a move and now all the humans here will suffer my recklessness.

I blink, my eyes remaining shut far longer than they should, and when I reopen them I see a pair of shiny black shoes advancing slowly. Zeus squats down, his knees cracking as he bends. "Amazingly brave, I will give you that, but are you sure that what you experienced is an illusion? Are you one hundred percent sure? Or can you feel your body losing its strength, your mind beginning to shut down? Can you feel yourself bleeding out? Many believe our minds are powerful enough to prevent our deaths, but can our minds also deliver death? I will be very interested to see."

"Maybe not today…" I whisper, and Zeus turns.

"What was that?"

My eyes roll open and then close, my voice now so ragged and low I'm unsure if he can hear me, but still I force myself to continue. "Maybe not today…maybe not tomorrow…but soon…someday soon…I am going to kill you."

And then before I can hear his response, my body surrenders to the pain. The last thing I remember is Lydian's voice inside my mind— *What have you done?*

CHAPTER 17

When I wake, Emmy is over me, easing something warm onto my forehead. She smiles wide when she sees me and presses her hand to my cheek. "We worry, child. We so worry."

I sit up in the bed and peer around, looking for Zeus, but all I see are the same empty walls I woke to a month ago. I'm back at the Panacea and by the expression on Emmy's face, I've been out for quite some time. "How long have I been here?" I ask.

"Few hours. Young-one be back any time now."

"How did I get here?" I search my thoughts for the last thing I remember. Zeus. I remember Zeus torturing me in the blue room, but there was someone else, someone I trusted, someone—

Jackson enters the room, his face fierce, and the memory comes flooding back. Jackson attacking me. Jackson pulling his knife on me. Jackson slicing my throat.

I jerk out of bed before I can rationalize that what I experienced before wasn't real. Jackson's eyes widen and he holds his hands out, as if I am a wild animal and he needs to reassure me that he means no harm.

"Ari…" he says, inching closer. I close my eyes, and suddenly he's lunging for me, strong and lethal. When I reopen them he's nearly to me, worry etched across his face. "What happened?"

I continue to back up, until a thought occurs to me. This is exactly what Zeus wanted. He intentionally picked Jackson as my attacker. He could have chosen anyone—any of the guards, anyone back on Earth, even himself—but he didn't. He chose Jackson, and he did it to create doubt in my mind. Regardless of what I'm feeling, I won't let Zeus mess with my head.

I force myself to take a step toward Jackson, force myself to keep my voice even, my expression blank. "Zeus restrained all the humans last night in their sleep. He killed that woman. He plans to kill again tomorrow. He…" I trail off, realizing how completely reckless I've behaved. I have no fear of death, so it was nothing for me to confront Zeus, plus I feel sure he won't kill me. But what about everyone else? The rest of the humans? They aren't safe here, especially when they can be used as punishment against me.

Cursing myself, I sit back on the bed and wrap my arms around my legs. "I messed up." I release a long, tired breath. "I attacked Zeus, so he put me in the blue room with a new attacker." I glance up at Jackson, watching as his expression changes from worry to anger to cautiousness. "You."

"He what?"

"My attacker in the…what is it? A simulation? Something more? Well, whatever it is, my attacker today was you and you sliced my throat. I thought I was bleeding to death. Was I?" I eye Emmy who pulls out her beads and runs them through her fingers and over each knuckle, deep in thought.

"He knows," she says.

Jackson stops on his way to me. "Knows what?"

"He knows Ari is going to be the one."

"The one what?" Jackson and I ask in unison.

Emmy turns to me, and I can tell that she doesn't want to tell me more. I feel the hesitation pouring off her. "What is it, Emmy?" I ask, growing worried. Something feels off. First Emmy has tried to train me to heal, then Mami asked to see me, all with the assumption that I was going to get everyone off Loge, but maybe it's more than that. "What do you know?"

"Some healers have deep skills. Some heal fast. Some mix remedies. And some, like me, see paths."

I cock my head at her as I sit up straight. "Emmy, I'm not foll—"

"I see you, child. I see where you were and where you go. I see what lies in your bones and what shakes your mind. I see you. And I see what you will do. Old-one see it, too. You not safe until we get you off this planet."

"Emmy…"

"Remember what you say to him last? He knows now, child. You're afraid, but tonight that will change. Strength will fuel you. Fear will subside. Now go home, rest. Lots to discover."

• • •

Jackson and I are walking the path around the river, a great distance from the Panacea, before either of us speaks. He opens his mouth to say something, but I already know what he is about to ask, so I cut him off, answering the question before it can leave his lips. "I told him that I was going to kill him." I cut my eyes over to him, hoping his reaction will show something that gives me courage. Instead, he lowers his head with a slight nod. "What are you thinking?" I ask, remembering how reckless Jackson had been after Mami was locked in the attic. It was the first time he let down his guard, and now I realize how far gone he really was to show so much of himself so freely. Now, I have no idea what he's thinking, even with the RES transmitter.

"You can always ask." Jackson glances over at me. "Ask me what I'm thinking."

I turn to him, our eyes meeting. "What are you thinking?"

He tucks a loose strand of hair behind my ear, lowering his hand so slowly it's as though it's painful for him to no longer touch me. "I'm thinking that I used to believe there was no such thing as fear. I taught myself a long time ago that while I might always have a reaction to Zeus that is something like fear, I would never let myself truly feel fear. I used to think that if you didn't fear death, then you were brave. I now know that it wasn't that I was fearless. It was that I didn't have anything to lose. Now I do." His eyes settle on mine, searching my face in a frantic sweep. "Now I know what it's like to be afraid, and I am. Petrified. I am so sick with fear that it consumes me. Because, as much as I hate the idea of Mami submitting to Zeus, at least I know that she will never intentionally get herself hurt. With you, I don't have that certainty. You don't know what he is capable of, Ari. Do I think that you are brave enough to try to kill him? Absolutely. Do I think you'll survive it?" He sighs. "No one ever has."

I reach out and take Jackson's hand in mine, needing either his comfort or to give him mine, I'm not sure. "I'm not planning to get myself killed. I'm smarter than that." I try to smile, to make light of the situation, but I know it's empty. Jackson tugs me closer to him, so close our faces are inches apart, and wraps his arms around me in a tight hug.

"Promise?" he whispers into my hair, and all I can do is nod, because we both know this isn't a promise I can keep. I've never been one to value my life over others and if it comes to it, in the end, I will always throw myself in first, regardless of the consequences. If my life saves the people here, then it is a very small price to pay, and one that I will gladly offer.

. . .

That night I'm startled awake by Vill standing over me. He presses a finger to his lips and motions for me to follow him out of my room. Jackson is sound asleep beside me, something we've fallen into that brings me too much comfort for me to push away. He no longer even asks. It's understood that at least for the night we can forget the complications of our days and just listen to each other's heartbeats until we fall asleep.

I follow Vill out of our room and down the hall to the door that leads to Jackson's office. He opens the door for me, and again doesn't step inside. "You have another call." And with that he shuts me inside. I edge down the stairs and into the bright room, my heart pounding. What if something happened back on Earth? What if something happened to Mom or Dad or Gretchen or Lawrence? I've barely spoken to them, and what if…? My thoughts cut short as my eyes focus on the screen.

On Gretchen.

I almost cry the moment my mind registers who it is. She looks different. Her hair is longer, which for Gretchen says enough. She has had the same chin-length hairstyle for years now, claiming the style defines her. Now her hair sweeps her shoulders. And her face, usually full of various bright shades of makeup, is bare. But that isn't what lets me know how rough things must be. Gretchen, even during difficult times, always looks put together. She dresses for the occasion—whatever the occasion may be—but right now she looks like either they woke her up in the middle of the night to come talk to me or she couldn't be bothered to put on anything other than junk clothes. The baggy gray T-shirt hangs awkwardly on her as though she borrowed it from someone two or three times her size and the black leggings have a hole in one of the knees. To anyone else, this wouldn't be concerning. So what if she decided to throw on whatever she could find and skipped makeup? She's just talking with me after all.

But I know better.

I press my hand to the screen and stare helplessly at her. Gretchen's bottom lip trembles as she raises her own to her screen and for a while we just stare at each other, both wishing we could talk like we used to. "I'm so glad to see you," I say finally. "I worried…" I don't want to admit that I thought she didn't care, because that's not the truth, not really. Still, I expected her to show in one of my chats with Law or for him to mention her or something.

She nods, tears building in her eyes. "I begged them to let me talk to you, Ari. I tried so hard. But they refused. I was at your last talk with Law though and I swear it took all of me to remain behind the screen. I hate this. I hate how they act as though—" Someone clears his or her throat in her room and she glances over the screen briefly before returning her gaze to me. "There are others in the room with me, Ari. I'm sure you already knew that, or at least guessed."

"I suspected as much," I say with a smile. "Who is with you?"

She looks over the screen again, and then apparently having received permission, says, "Law, your dad, and Interim President Lancaster."

"Gretchen, what has happened to President Cartier?"

At this her eyes flash back over the screen and then to me twice before settling down.

"Gretch…? Has something happened to Sandra?"

Before she can answer Law and my dad join her in chairs in front of her screen. Seeing them all together should give me a sense of comfort. It doesn't. They all show signs of exhaustion and worry.

"Ari," Dad says, taking the lead, "Sandra has had a stroke.

The medics believe she will recover fully in time, but for now we have had to make concessions."

"Like what? Who is leading Parliament?"

"Kelvin and I have stepped in to assist, with the help of Lawrence as he is not yet of age to fully accept his role."

My eyes drift over to Lawrence, and suddenly I realize that was the change I noticed in him. He no longer has his trademark easiness, instead trading it for a look that can only be described as presidential. I wonder what really goes on within his mind and if he's as terrified as I imagine him to be.

"I'm sorry," I say to him. "I hope she recovers soon."

Law dips his head in acknowledgment, but doesn't say anything further about her. "We ran extensive analysis on the connection here and it appears to be safe. Whoever created it did amazing work."

"That's Vill. We've hacked into an old satellite here to tap into your satellite. Zeus isn't monitoring the old one…for now. Vill's insanely intelligent. You would like him, I think," I say, though with Law acting so serious it feels like an inappropriate comment. For a moment his gaze holds on mine and I think I see the ghost of a smile on his lips, but then it's gone, replaced by the empty expression I've grown used to seeing from him. The thought of it makes me sad, and I have to look away to keep myself from telling him so.

"How is Cybil and the other humans?" Dad asks, and I launch into everything that I've seen and speculated on. I tell him about them hanging the woman today off the bridge, and stop when I notice them nodding.

"We saw," Gretchen says. "It was broadcast on the T-screens. Zeus can somehow break into our frequency whenever he likes. We saw you, too." Gretchen looks down.

I glare at Kelvin. "Then why did you allow it to happen? Didn't you at least try to negotiate?"

"Of course we tried," Kelvin says. "There is no compromising with Zeus. We can't allow him to come here."

I jump up, my anger taking over. "Well, while you're trying to come up with a solution, people are dying here. Another death is scheduled for tomorrow morning. Their blood is on your hands."

"Ari, calm down." Dad's expression shifts from his typical commander look to that of my dad. Worried, afraid for me.

"Zeus has been asking me about an entrance. What is he talking about?"

Dad opens his mouth to respond, but Kelvin silences him with one look. "We are unable to discuss that here. Security measures. I'm sure you understand."

I glance from person to person. Kelvin, emotionless and cold. Dad, worried and angry. Gretchen, chewing on her nails, her bottom lip quivering. But it's Law who actually speaks, "It all comes down to Zeus, Ari."

"Which brings us to the point of this call," Kelvin says. "How is your progress?"

I sigh. "We've had…complications. I have a plan that I feel sure will work. I just need more time."

Kelvin laces his hands together and leans forward. "There is no time. You know what to do." And then before I can respond, he nods to someone out of sight, and the screen goes dark.

CHAPTER 18

I crawl back into bed beside Jackson, though I know there is no way I'll sleep. I'm surprised that he slept the entire time I was gone. He has a peacefulness about him when he sleeps, an easy rise and fall to his chest, and the slowest, deepest breaths, each one as though he's breathing a small sigh of relief. I watch him like this, wondering what he would think about my talking to Earth's leaders without him knowing.

His eyes flutter a little, the tell-tale sign of REM sleep, and I wonder what dreams he's walking through right now and whether any of them include me. He said he had no fear prior to his feelings for me, but for me it's the opposite. I used to be afraid. Afraid of expectation and what it meant to be Ari Alexander, whether I would ever live up to my own name. Now, I have no fear. Not of losing the ones I love or war or even of becoming something other than what I've always been. And I know that part of becoming okay with myself and the future, no matter where it takes me, is because of Jackson. On Earth he taught me that there was a world outside of what I had always known. Now here, on Loge, he's taught me that even the strongest, most guarded people have a vulnerable side.

I pushed Jackson away, yet he continues to stand beside me, forever thinking I am better than I am, more capable than I am—stronger than I am. Some may think you choose to have feelings for another due to what you see in that person, their strengths and weaknesses. But I think it's also in how that person sees you. And Jackson Castello, right or wrong, sees me, really sees me. How can I push that away? How can I deny that while I see him as mysterious and difficult, I also see him as kind and generous and so much braver than he realizes? He isn't perfect. He is so far from perfect. But maybe it isn't about him being perfect…maybe it's about him being perfect for me.

I shiver as the thought circulates through me, each second making me realize the truth of it all. Jackson is perfect for me.

I slip under the covers beside him and edge closer, feeling both anxious and excited at the same time. Looking down on him, I've never seen anyone more beautiful in my entire life, and I wish I could guarantee he was always at peace, just like this. And then the reality of everything hits me—the impending war, my plan against Zeus, the risks that may end up burying me—and I no longer feel that time is on my side. I'm tired of allowing my mind to fight my heart. I lean down until my breath dances with his and close my eyes, allowing my lips to caress his so lightly it's barely a touch, but the impact is immediate. He jars awake, and I slowly open my eyes to see his staring, surprised, into mine.

"I thought you were asleep," I whisper.

"Clearly I am." And then in one move he cups my face with his hands and sits us up, crushing his lips onto mine. I pull him still closer, wanting my body as fixed to his as possible, finding strength in his powerful arms and the sureness of his kiss, as though he was always here, waiting for this moment. He eases me down onto the bed and lies half over me, never letting his lips leave mine. A small tear leaks from my eye and I realize that for the first time since arriving here, I feel like I'm coming home.

Jackson pulls away, his expression full of confusion as he wipes away the tear. "Did I—?"

"No. This is…you're…" I swallow the lump in my throat and try to steady my voice. "I'm sorry it took me so long to get here, to realize…"

Jackson places a finger over my mouth to stop me. "Don't apologize. You could never forgive me or talk to me again, and it would change nothing for me. Still, my first thought every day for the rest of my life…will be you."

I choke on a sob that feels like it's been pent up inside me forever. I cry for everything I've lost and everything I didn't realize I had. I cry for what I have done and what I am about to do. But most of all, I cry because this shattered boy has carried my weight for weeks now, reassuring me and supporting me, while also fighting the horrors that Zeus inflicts upon him, and I continually pushed him away.

Jackson slides beside me, curling me up against him and rubbing my back gently until the sobs turn into easier breaths and my tears dry on my face. Exhausted, I melt into him, listening as his heart beats against my cheek, until finally we both fall fast asleep.

CHAPTER 19

The next morning I stretch my arms out in bed to find the space beside me empty and for a moment I wonder if I dreamt the whole thing. I crawl out of bed and leave the room to hear the shower running from the back door.

Glad for a moment to think, I get dressed and head out to the front porch. In a few hours, another human is going to die. I feel my stomach sink at the thought, my mind searching for a way that I can stop it. People are already in motion, walking down the central street of our row to Gaia Road to go to work or school or whatever. I stand and walk the opposite way down the street, immersing myself in the flow of people. They are all harmless, just wanting to go about their lives. I wonder how easy it will be to convince them, how many would stand up against Zeus.

I walk back down to our house to find Jackson waiting on the porch for me. "Do you want to go to the bridge?"

I lace my fingers behind my head and close my eyes. "No. But how can I not?"

A few minute later and we're standing by the bank to the Cutana River, a crowd already forming. The guards line both sides of the bridge, pushing onlookers back. From this vantage point, it's hard to see who Zeus has chosen to sacrifice today. I scan the crowd, the bridge, the guards, trying to work out possible ways in my mind that I can stop this.

"You can't," Jackson whispers, pulling me close. "You can't stop this."

I bite my lip, torn between what I have to do, the many who could be saved, and this single life about to be taken before me. Is one life worth saving many? And if it is, how do you determine the worth of that life? I feel a deep ache in my chest that I know will never completely go away. There has been so much death in this war, so much loss.

I drop my head and close my eyes. I don't want to watch it happen, knowing there is nothing I can do to stop it. Several seconds pass and I hear a cry move through the crowd. My eyes dart to the bridge and I have to stifle my own cry. Perched on the edge of the railing is a boy, no older than ten or twelve. His small body is shaking, and though he isn't crying, I can see his fear, feel it radiating off him.

I take a step forward just as someone screams from the crowd, "You can't do this!" Then more shouts of, "He's just a boy!" and "He didn't do anything!" The guard behind the boy sneers, and I decide in that moment that if he pushes that boy off the bridge, I will kill him. I will kill him and I will enjoy it.

Jackson steps around me, composed, but I can tell he's prepared to fight if he has to. He reaches the guard and begins to argue with him, motioning to the boy and then up at Zeus's building where the coward no doubt watches this with joy. The crowd begins to get angrier and angrier as we wait for the decision.

I step away from the crowd, closer to the river, and the boy's eyes fall on me, helpless and afraid. And that's enough for me. I turn so I'm facing the majority of the people and shout as loudly as I can, "You don't have to allow this! You don't have to watch him kill this little boy. You are a strong group. You can rise above. You *can* fight back!"

A series of assents course through the crowd, and soon Ancients are pushing and yelling, some trying to make their way to the boy, others trying to hold them back. A fight breaks out, then another, and soon it's full out madness as the Ancients divide, those willing to stand against Zeus and those too loyal to allow it.

The guards have all moved into the crowd to break up the fighting, giving us our only chance of freeing the boy. I scream, "Jackson!" and motion to the boy. Jackson starts for him, he's almost there, when a shot rings out through the air and the boy, startled, falls forward to the water, the noose around his neck jerking him to a stop. His body writhes and jerks as he tries to find ground that isn't there. Jackson pulls a knife from his pocket and begins to cut the rope, but it's too thick, the boy too small to sustain. I rush into the water and swim with all my might against the current to try to reach him.

"I've got it," Jackson shouts, and the boy's body falls into the water. A wave of relief surges through me. We saved him. We saved him! I pull the boy from the water and lift him up onto the shore, prepared to give CPR if necessary, when my eyes land on the boy's face, blue and lifeless.

"Oh, no." I pump his chest and breathe into his mouth, praying it isn't too late, even though deep in my chest, I know he's gone. I continue issuing CPR until my arms are aching and my breath has become labored, only stopping when someone places a hand on my shoulder.

"Ari, he's gone. I'm sorry. He's gone."

Tears brim my eyes, and I look up to see Madison beside me, her face soaked from crying. She kneels down beside me, and wraps me in a tight hug. "I'm sorry."

Everything inside me crashes in that moment, torn between absolute anger and absolute defeat. More guards appear, ordering people to their homes, forcing the crowd to disperse. Jackson arrives and helps me stand, and at some point tells me we have to go home, but I'm too lost to listen. Because though I know the image of the boy will stay ingrained in my mind for the rest of my life, something happened today that I never could have anticipated. The Ancients spoke out. They fought. They rallied together for the greater good. Which means hope isn't lost. I don't have to start a rebellion.

It's already begun.

. . .

Instantly, it's as though the air is different, the sky ominous, as though Loge itself knows what I plan to do and intends to stop me from killing its leader. Jackson and I walk together down Gaia Road an hour later, hand in hand. It's another change, this one such a source of strength that I'm amazed I pushed him away for so many weeks. I want him near me, always near me, because I know as long as he's there I have someone on my side who, like me, fears failing more than death.

The guards blocked all the streets for an hour after the uprising at the river, forcing everyone to stay in their homes. Jackson and I talked about nothing but the plan the entire time we were home. What we would do and when and how, and by the end of the hour, we had everything sorted out.

The Earthly port is monitored by guards that switch out every four hours, except during the middle of the night, when they go a six hour stretch. The switch at that six hour mark takes the longest because the guards are exhausted and most of Triad is still asleep. Our plan is to have the Ancients who want to leave slip outside the Healer's Wall and come around to where the wall meets the Taking Forest. They can then come in through the Taking Forest and go through the Earthly port. We will have apprehended the guards by then, giving them free clear to go without worry of harm. We'll block the port from any potential threat, and then go for Zeus. But to make this happen, we need all of the human Operatives and at least some of the RESs to ally with us against Zeus.

Which brings us to our goal for today: recruiting anti-Zeus soldiers.

"You remember the plan?" Jackson says out of the corner of his mouth. No one is around, but that doesn't mean no one is listening.

I nod. The plan is for Jackson to go to Cybil and have her spread the word to the Operatives about the rebellion, set to occur two nights from tonight. I will then discreetly mention it to the RES assignees, in hopes that they are less ingrained with Zeus and will be more willing to help.

Jackson and I separate as soon as we enter the Vortex, him down the spiral steps to see Cybil, me through the double doors to RES training. Most of the RESs are standing around talking when I enter. Madison rushes up to me. "Are you okay? That was so horrible."

One of the male assignees behind her overhears and calls, "We can't allow this to continue." A conversation starts before I even have to utter a word. I smile to myself, proud for the first time to call myself an RES.

"I can get us all back to Earth, if you're willing to help," I finally say, breaking up the conversations. They turn to me, intrigue in their eyes, and I launch into the plan. I keep my voice low to prevent any wandering ears from hearing. We talk about Earth's leaders allowing coexistence, about the Ancients who want to leave, about the humans who are slated to die here, and by the time I'm done, I have them all in agreement.

Jackson comes through the door just as I'm finishing up, his arms loaded down with metal boxes. He sets the boxes on the ground and steps up to the group. "Today you will each receive your RX-53."

"But I thought we didn't receive our guns until next year," a male Ancient calls. "You're giving them early?"

"I'm giving them early."

Jackson passes each of the Ancients a gun, and then when he gets to me he hands mine over and whispers, "Cybil is on board.

"All right," he says, addressing the group. "Everyone know how to use it?" He walks over to the stack of wooden wheels from our first training, and holds the gun out so everyone can see. He cocks it, then clicks a red button on the side that begins to flash. Then he tosses the wheel into the air and fires, sending a burst of light at the wheel, shattering it into a million pieces. "That's it. Now practice. I want this room covered in splinters when I return." He leaves the room, and we stare at one another for a moment, then the Operative in me takes over and I head for a wheel, glancing at one of the male Ancients as I go.

"You toss them for the group. We'll go one after the other. Sound good?" Everyone nods and gets into line. I start, remembering my first Operative training back home. We were put into lines, similar to this, and fired at various targets until we hit all of them. I remember Jackson being asked to illustrate for the group, and then the awe in everyone's eyes as we were handed a new prototype laser gun. It was so powerful, so advanced. And it was nothing compared to the gun I hold in my hand now.

Its smooth silver lines help it to fit perfectly in my hand. It's so light that I assume the blast will be weak, so when I fire, I'm not expecting the kick that sends me backward onto the ground. I feel a tingling sensation in my hand and shake my head to refocus my thoughts. At least I hit the wheel, which is now scattered across the other side of the room, like Jackson's from before. I expect the group to laugh at my fall, but instead Madison helps me stand and they all continue shooting, each of them focused, and I realize the events of the morning have hit deep. They're angry. They're motivated.

They're ready to fight.

CHAPTER 20

I leave the Vortex filled with excitement and new determination. Eager to find Jackson, I circle around to the back of the Vortex where he said he would be working with RES soldiers. I almost pop out from the side of the building, when instead I decide to watch them. Jackson has them stacked in rows and they're all wearing uniforms and holding weapons that are unlike anything I've ever seen before. Jackson calls out a few commands and they march. He calls out another set of commands and they stop. They do this over and over and then he calls out once more and they turn in unison and fire into the air, but where I expect shots to ring out or a laser or something at all familiar, I see a burst that looks exactly like a lightning bolt on a hot summer day just before a massive thunderstorm rolls in to cool off the land. The bolts have an intelligence about them, dying out as soon as they hit the air, as though they know there isn't a true target in sight and they can reserve their energy for a more useful time.

"Spy!" someone calls from behind me, startling me so much that when I'm pushed from behind the building, all I can do is stumble. I spin around, preparing to punch, when Mackenzie's devilish laugh hits my ears, followed by her usual mocking expression. "What are you doing hiding over here, human?" She pushes me again, and this time there is no way I'm holding back. I lunge forward, sweeping her feet out from under her so she lands hard on her back. I am about to give her a chance to apologize when Jackson grabs me.

"What are you doing?" Then he whispers low in my ear. "Calm down, Ari. You know this is what he wants." And he's right. Mackenzie is nothing more than Zeus's minion, sent around to do his bidding. Letting her get to me is just allowing him to have control.

"Nothing," I say, brushing off my pants as though they are covered in dirt. "I was just looking for you, but I saw that you were busy so I was preparing to head back home when this twit spotted me."

Jackson glances over his shoulder. All the RESs are watching us now. He gives me a pointed look, so full of concern it is almost a caress, and then directs his anger at Mackenzie. "Either get in line or get out of here. You're distracting my troop."

Mackenzie smiles the devilish grin she's perfected around me. "I was sent for her."

Jackson crosses his arms. "Fine. I'm coming, too."

"You know better," I say. "I'll see you later." And with that I follow her to Zeus.

Mackenzie walks me the entire way to Zeus's office, as though I need an escort, and I instantly get the feeling something has changed. Zeus is standing by the window when I enter his office, his right arm over his head, resting against the smooth glass. From this angle he looks like a normal person, nowhere near the predator that I know he is. At this thought, he smiles and turns around. "Ah, so nice to see you too, Ari dear. Please sit." He motions to a chair in front of his desk and then turns back to the window. "I hear you and my grandson have grown close. Did you know Jackson once loved another? I'm betting not. In fact, I bet he's never mentioned her at all."

I swallow back the rush of emotions threatening to burst to the surface. This is what he wants, to rattle me. Why else would he bring up Jackson's past as though it has anything to do with the present?

"Oh doesn't it?" Zeus says as he walks toward me. He snatches a glass full of a ruby liquid from his desk that I know must be a Healer concoction. Maybe some herb or flower that keeps him alive well past the typical lifespan of an Ancient. Or maybe something that makes it where he is stronger than others, more intelligent than others, who knows. He grins wide at my rambling thoughts and runs a finger over the rim of the glass. "It's Hyptotica. And it isn't for me. It's for you." As soon as the words leave his mouth, two Ancient guards come in through a side door and stand on my right and left. "But you're right; it is a healer's brew created especially for me in times like these. See, I'm growing tired, Ari. Something is happening back on Earth. I feel it in my blood, just as I'm sure most Ancients do on some level."

I glance at the guards and slowly widen my stance. "I don't understand."

Zeus laughs. "Of course not. Your mind operates under exact truths, but where we are concerned, there has never been a truth given to humans. Surely you never believed that we only Took antibodies from you and that is why we continued the Taking for all those years? We possess xylem. Why would we need antibodies to keep us alive on Earth?"

He smiles. "Sure, there would be an acclimation period. With so many parasites and bacteria on Earth, our bodies could not heal them all quickly enough to keep us strong. We would be too vulnerable. So yes, we Took antibodies to speed up our acclimation. But that was never why the Taking existed."

He pauses in front of me, the glass sparkling in the light from the chandelier above us. "The Taking was created to give us knowledge of how you work—your mind, your body, your thoughts, your emotions. Every element of the human structure delivered to us like computerized code. We Took from you so we could understand our enemy. And now we know what we are up against. The problem is there is a break in the code. I'm getting bits of information that make no sense. So, you will be providing the information I need. Of course I know of your most recent rally with my troops." He cocks his head to the left and studies my face with curiosity. "Though you already knew that, didn't you? I have no idea what you are up to, but trust that your most driven endeavors," he says, his voice shaking, then, "endeavors: an attempt to achieve a goal, are no match for mine. Now drink."

I take a step away from the drink and feel the guards' hands lock on my arms to stop me. "I'm not drinking that or anything else."

Zeus smirks, leaning down to smell the brew. "Oh I think you will. As I was saying earlier, you are not Jackson's first venture into love. Like Katalina you possess far too much feist. And like Katalina you are destined to end up in the ground." He steps forward, thrusting the drink to my lips. "Now drink, else I should put you there today. The only reason I allow you to live is because you provide a usefulness to me that no other human here can possess. Once that usefulness is worn out, you will be handled."

I lock my lips together, but the pressure of the glass against my mouth and the guards' hold on me forces my lips to split enough for Zeus to tip the drink back. It stings the moment it hits my tongue, burning like flamed lava down my throat. I expect something to happen, some force to render me helpless or void of emotion, something that gives Zeus control. But nothing happens.

"Sit," Zeus says, pointing at the chair again, and something in the command tells me he expects me to follow it now. Confusion cloaks my mind. One of the healers made this brew especially for Zeus to use on me. Would she intentionally make it so it doesn't work? Emmy would for sure. And then there is Lydian, though I have never counted her as a friend. Still, something was there at the last torture session. She was worried about me, afraid.

Tension builds in my chest as I try to figure out how I should behave and what I should say. I shut down my mind, clearing it except for what is around me. I picture the guards, Zeus, his office, anything to keep my mind from drifting.

"What have you given me?"

Zeus leans back in his chair. "Consider it your daily dose of truth. You will come to me every day. You will drink that drink. And you will willingly offer me any information that I may ask. Our sessions in the blue room are not providing the results I need. But this will."

I scowl, wishing I had spit the drink out or fought harder to avoid drinking it. What if I unveil the plan or something about Jackson? What if I reveal that Mami has been to see me? Many could get hurt. I try to feel a change in my mind, my body, my blood pressure, something that hints that the drink has taken effect, but again come up empty. Though maybe there is no change, only a trigger in my mind that forces me to tell Zeus the truth no matter what he asks. I look at the ground as I try to calm my mind. Zeus can't know that I'm worried.

"Well, go ahead," I say, glancing up. "Give it a go."

He links his fingers in front of him, tapping the wrinkled index fingers together as though to some unheard rhythm.

"You are not fond of me, are you?"

"Am I that obvious?" I say.

Zeus's face twists. "Tell me about your Chemists. Are they capable of developing a weapon against us?"

Again I search for some hint that the drink is working, that I'm about to blurt out all of our secrets, but nothing comes. If it was indeed Lydian, she put herself at a great risk to do this for me. She expects me to keep Zeus from reading my mind and knowing the brew didn't work. I close my eyes briefly, pushing all thought from my mind, then answer. "They are capable of virtually anything. So yes, I would say a weapon is more than possible." I hate that I'm admitting this to him, but surely he realizes this himself. Of course the Chemists are capable of advanced weaponry. Whether those weapons could succeed is another question altogether.

"And are you in communication with them currently?" Zeus asks, and I hear the hint of something in his voice that tells me he suspects Jackson and I have a means, he just isn't sure how we did it.

I steady my gaze on his. "Don't you think you would know if I were communicating with them? Further, don't you think if it were possible for me to communicate with them, I would already be there, not here?"

My heart threatens to expose me the moment the words leave my mouth. Zeus considers the answer for so long that I'm sure he knows, sure he's about to order the guard to kill me, or worse, that he's going to kill someone else for my actions. But then his face relaxes, if only marginally. "So be it." He walks to his desk, opens the top drawer, and pulls out two metal balls. "Take them," he says. I shake my head and the guards force my hands open and then closed around both balls. He nods to one of the guards, who cocks his gun and points it at my head. "Drop them and I order him to shoot. Do you understand?"

I nod, suddenly afraid.

Zeus sits at his desk across from me and leans forward, his eyes trainined on mine. "Where is the entrance?"

"I don't know," I answer, then feel a jolt rush into my palms, stinging its way up my arms. I start to drop the metal balls, when Zeus eyes the guard on my left, and he presses his gun to my temple.

"If you release them, he shoots."

"I don't know what you're talking about. I don't know of an entrance."

Zeus lifts his hand from the desk to show a tiny metal piece in his hand with a clickable button at the top. "Very well." He presses the button and the jolt intensifies, climbing my forearms and shaking my shoulders. Tears prick my eyes from the pain, and I grit my teeth together, praying the shock will end. I let out a loud breath as it stops, wondering for the first time in my life if it's possible to die of pain alone.

"I am half Ancient. Do you really think they would have told me?"

Zeus considers this for some time, then stands and motions for the door. "We shall see. I have business to attend. You will report to Lydian for the remainder of your questioning. I will see you back here tomorrow. If you truly don't know the location, then I will use you as leverage. One way or another, I will learn the location of the entrance."

• • •

I'm out the main doors of the Castello building, in a full sprint to our house, my mind a whirlwind of worry that I can't contain. I have so much to do and so little time. I burst through the front door, covering each room in search of Jackson before finally finding him in our room, luggage packed on the end of the bed.

"What's that?" I ask as I near, everything about it making me feel all the more uncomfortable.

He sits beside it and pulls me into his lap. "Zeus wants to make a round of visits at the other regions. We head out tonight."

"But why do you have to go with him? How long will you be gone?"

"I always go. It would look suspicious if I tried to stay. We'll be gone two days. He wants to make sure they're ready. It's getting close. Dangerous." He places his hands on either side of my face, hesitating, then says, "I want you to leave here with the others. I'll get to Earth somehow. Don't worry about killing Zeus, just leave. Before it gets bad. Law will be ready. You don't have to stay here and—"

"No," I say, stopping him. "This changes nothing. I'm not leaving you behind. I can't. And with Zeus still in place, we're all in danger. He has to be killed."

Jackson looks away uneasily.

"I can do this." I hold his gaze, fighting against the hurt in my voice. "Don't lose faith in me."

"Never." He pulls me in to him, his arms tight around me, cradling me with his strength and in them I feel what he refuses to say. This may be the last peaceful moment we have, the last sense of comfort or normalcy. I want to melt into him, lay with him until he's forced to leave, but I'm too much my father's daughter to waste precious strategizing time on my own selfish wants, so I pull myself away, kissing him easily on the lips before standing.

"I'll have everything in place before you get back. Just get to the port as soon as you can. If luck is on our side, everyone will cross over before the rest of the RESs realize anything has happened."

Jackson leans back on the heels of his hands. "You underestimate them. The only hope you have is that your troop can hold long enough for most to cross, though even that is hoping for a lot. You need to prepare yourself, Ari. Most of the humans are going to die in this fight."

I walk over to the window and peer out over Triad, tranquil, no hint of the fight that is about to erupt. "No, you underestimate the human heart. These people have loved ones back home. Husbands and wives and children. Brothers and sisters and parents. They have friends and family who miss them. They aren't going to just lie down."

"They aren't fighters, Ari."

"You'd be surprised what people become when they have no other choice."

Jackson comes up behind me and kisses the top of my head. "I hope you're right."

CHAPTER 21

I go to Lydian, eager to see for myself which side she is on. Jackson left me with one request: Avoid anything overly dangerous until he returns. I have to wonder if he felt the words were a waste before he said them. After all, he knows I will do nothing less than what is necessary—dangerous or not.

Lydian is already waiting behind the glass when I arrive in the blue room, her expression full of worry. *Yes. I altered the brew,* she says into my mind before I can ask. *I know what you plan to do. I want to help...if you will let me.*

"How do I know if I can trust you?"

She shrugs. "You could ask that question of anyone. I guess you have to decide for yourself. But Mami and I have developed a plan that may help you. Zeus drinks a mind vial daily to maintain his mental strength. I brew it for him and give him enough for his weekly consumption. I restocked his supply this morning. Instead of his normal brew, I have altered the concoction so it slows down the mind, his reflexes, everything. It is a gradual thing so he isn't likely to notice for a few days."

I walk closer to the glass. "I don't understand. Why would you help me? He'll know you did it. He's too smart to think it's a coincidence. He'll know and he'll kill you for it. I can't let you—"

She tosses up her hands to stop me. "I am already dead here, Ari. He treats us as though we are his property, disposable at any time. I can't live like this any longer, I won't. Just promise me one thing." I wait, afraid of what she is about to say, when she says, "My daughter—Madison. Take her with you. I can't let her suffer the way I have, the way all healers suffer. Promise me you will take her with you and I will do whatever I can to guarantee your success."

Madison. I knew her mother was a healer, but I had no idea her mother was Lydian. I wonder if Lydian has talked about me to Madison. I wonder if she knows that her mother has been torturing me.

I glance up to see the certainty in her face. I knew Zeus had made enemies here, but I never imagined so many Logeans would betray him. When I left Earth, I felt sure humans were in the wrong, and while I didn't trust Zeus, I thought he at least had the Logean's best interests in mind. Now I know Zeus only cares about winning. He no longer cares about anything other than destroying humans, which makes it all that much easier to convince myself that he deserves to be dead.

I fix my gaze on her, my body filled with a new resolve. "I promise," I say, the words more than just a sentiment to Lydian that I will protect her daughter. I'm making a promise to myself, because at the end of the day I have no idea how bad this fight will get, no idea what shape Earth will be in when we return. Law says we will be safe, that the neurotoxin has diminished, but what if he's wrong? What if I bring these people there just to watch them die?

Lydian's eyes turn soft. "Trust yourself, child. We do. Now go. Emmy is waiting for you."

. . .

Emmy is sitting on the bench between the gardens and the Taking Forest when I arrive. She doesn't look up, though I know she senses me nearing. I sit beside her and she reaches out to take my hand. "Thank you for coming."

"Of course. What is it, Emmy? Is something wrong?"

She grips my hand tighter. "You will act when he returns, yes?"

I nod.

"And you are prepared to do what you must?"

I swallow. "I'm prepared to die if that is what you mean."

At this she turns to me and grips the sides of my head hard. "Then take this." A force surrounds my head and I pull and jerk against Emmy to try to free myself from the pain.

"Emmy, stop. Stop!" I claw at her hands, but her fingers lock down still tighter around my head. My body begins to shake from the pressure, my vision blurring. "E-mmy."

"Take it!" she screams.

Suddenly it's as though a crack, a tiny sliver of light, bursts from my scull and little by little the force around my head seeps through the crack, warming my mind, my eyes, my nose, my ears, heightening my senses to the point that I feel as though I am no longer trapped by my body, but free in the air, experiencing everything at once. All sounds, all smells, all feelings. I gasp as Emmy releases me, and I fall back against the bench. "What did you do?" I ask, breathless.

"I gave you some of me."

I glimpse up at Emmy. She looks tired, older. "I don't understand," I say, closing my eyes. I feel jittery, as though I've taken too many energy shots.

Emmy takes my hand again, patting it in the way she does that always brings me comfort. "You needed to heal, so now you can." I open my eyes and stare into hers, a strange beat in my chest that hits in opposition to my heart, like a second heartbeat. And suddenly I realize what she's telling me. Emmy has just breathed life into me, as she would for one of the flowers in the garden, but with her breath of life, she gave me a greater gift—she gave me her ability to heal.

"I don't know what to say."

Emmy smiles. "Say nothing. Now you're ready."

CHAPTER 22

An hour and a half later, I find myself sitting in front of the communicator screen in Jackson's office, waiting for Law. I need to be sure before I move forward that we have the same agenda. The last thing I want is to bring Logeans to Earth just to have them killed or thrown into execution chambers. I came here the moment I left Emmy and have been staring at a blank screen ever since.

"Come on, Law," I say under my breath. "Be there. Come on." But still only silence greets me. I pull my legs in tight in the chair and rest my forehead on my knees. I have two days to kill Zeus, two days to get everyone to Earth. Thinking through everything I have to do is enough to cause my mind to want to shut down, though I know I don't have time for a mental breakdown. I don't have time for worry or fear or anything other than action. That's the only way I have a chance of succeeding, and I have no choice but to succeed.

"Ari?"

My eyes snap to the screen, but instead of Law, Gretchen stares back at me. "Gretch?" Her face is creased with concern and she looks tired, like days-of-no-sleep tired. "What's happened?" I ask as I scoot closer to the screen.

She looks around, though I can't see anyone else in the room. "I don't know how long I have. They wouldn't—"

"Gretchen."

"I'm not supposed—"

"Gretchen."

"It could be—"

"Gretchen!"

Her head jerks straight, her eyes wide.

"Just tell me what's going on."

"We're told Zeus will be attacking in less than a week. They're taking…preventative measures."

I stand, coming closer to the screen as though being closer will help me get something more out of what she is saying. "I don't understand. Preventative…?"

"They are shutting down this communication, Ari. We're not supposed to talk to you. It's dangerous. Things are getting intense here."

"I don't understand. You can't talk to me? What about the plan? Has it changed? I'm helping to get everyone back home. I need to know it's safe there for them. Please…tell me it's safe."

Gretchen glances around again. She's so nervous, too nervous. What has happened there to make her so afraid? And where is Law? Where is Dad?

"Gretchen?"

Her eyes settle on mine, her expression more frightened than I've ever seen her. "No one is safe."

"What?"

Static fills the air and the screen blurs in and out of focus, black and white lines running through the image. "Can you hear me? What's happening? Gretchen?" I grip the sides of the screen, panic searing my chest.

"Ari?" The screen flashes—static, Gretchen, static,

Gretchen. She's close to the screen, her voice a whisper of terror. "Ari, are you there? If you can hear me, don't—"

And then she's gone.

CHAPTER 23

"She didn't say anything else?" Cybil asks as we make our way out to the field before her training. The Operatives have reached a sort of half citizenship in Triad. They can come and go as long as they communicate where they're going and with whom. The rest of the humans are on lockdown, their existence now tied to Zeus's threat to Earth's leaders.

I went to see Cybil the moment I was sure Gretchen wasn't returning. I tried again and again to reconnect to Earth, to get someone—anyone—to answer me, but after an hour I knew the connection was gone and whatever had Gretchen so rattled had begun on Earth. My mind is filled with worry and dread. We can't stay on Loge, not with the planet dying and Zeus growing crazier by the second. Even if I'm successful and I kill him, we are still living on a planet that is ticking toward its death.

"No, the screen went black. There was static at first, and then nothing, as though someone pulled the plug. She was afraid, Cybil. Really afraid. And something tells me her fears were deeper than just what Zeus is planning. I think she's afraid of someone there. Or maybe what they plan to do. I'm not sure. Do you have any idea what they could be planning?"

Cybil stops in the grass and glances around. "There was once talk of moving everyone below ground and releasing toxins into the air that would make the surface unlivable for a year. Operatives would stay above to fight just in case there were Ancients that were able to make it past the toxins. The thought was that Loge would be dead by then and Zeus would have no choice but to find another planet to inhabit. The problem was that it would take time to build a fully contained belowground environment and we didn't have time."

"That might be what Zeus is wanting when he keeps asking me about an entrance. Maybe he knows they're belowground and wants to know how to breach their hideaway. And maybe that's why the connection was lost. Surely they couldn't get as good of a frequency belowground."

Cybil shakes her head. "No. That wouldn't have been a problem. They had worked through all ways of communicating so we could stay in contact with the other Trinities. This is something else."

"Do you think it's safe there?"

She shrugs. "As safe as it is here."

I swallow hard, letting the truth of her words sink in. These people, the Logeans, none of them want to fight. Back on Earth, I thought I had to choose a side. I thought either the Ancients were good or the humans were good. It didn't seem possible that maybe there were bad and good within each group and that like with any war throughout history, the people—the everyday people—were the truly good ones and the ones to suffer the most. I realize in that moment that I will never be a commander to the Engineers or a commander to a Logean army. Not after everything I've seen. From now on my role, my job, is to protect the lives of those who are unable to protect themselves, the humans and Logeans who have no stake in this war beyond their goal to live through it. I am their commander. And I will not fail them.

"Deep thought?" Cybil asks as she walks up beside me.

I glance over at Cybil. "We need to talk about what to do once we're back on Earth. Do we head for Business Park to see Dad? Keep everyone in the woods until we know it's safe? The port should drop us into the woods, but what if it doesn't? Again, we should think through—"

"Ari…"

"What?"

"What if they have gone underground? What then? We have no way of communicating with Lawrence or your dad. Anyone left on the surface will be told to shoot first, ask questions later. They aren't going to care who we are—or who we were to them. We need to prepare for the fact that we may leave an attack here only to go into a full out war."

A sick feeling swirls through my core, settling there as though I've eaten something that doesn't agree with my system. She's right. This whole time I've envisioned Sydia exactly as we left it, familiar like an old friend, when it could be a stranger to me now. I have to go there assuming I have no allies. I have to go there assuming the war will begin the moment our feet touch land.

"I'm going to meet with Emmy, Lydian, and Mami to finalize their part of the plan. The Operatives all all set, right?"

"Yes, half are leading the Ancients and humans outside the Healer's Wall to the Taking Forest. The other half will help you defend the port. What about the assignees?"

"They're ready. I sent a message to each of them on where to be and when. We're all ready. Think you could spy on the RESs a bit? Find out what their attack strategy is on Earth?"

"Sure, but couldn't you just ask Jackson when he returns?"

I shake my head and glance around again. Something in the air feels off. Night has settled in, bringing with it a light breeze that moves around us like a ghost, eager to learn our deepest secrets. "I don't think Zeus would tell him. He's using Jackson to train them, sure, but it's almost as though Jackson is just a tool. I'm betting Zeus gave them orders to follow while he's away with Jackson. And I'm betting Jackson going with him has nothing to do with him being the next leader. He wanted Jackson away from Triad. Why? There has to be a reason."

Cybil considers this for a moment, and then sighs. "Okay, but I'm taking a weapon."

I grin and pluck a flower from the ground at my feet, watching as it blooms in my hand, my touch sparking life into it. "I wouldn't expect anything less."

CHAPTER 24

Instead of taking the main path, I go around the Vortex and cut through the small patch of woods that surround Zeus's house, where they requested we meet. The trees are different here; though they still have bark and are brown with green leaves, their shape is different, the branches twisting awkwardly and painfully as though they were broken bones that weren't properly set before healing. I press my palm to the trunk of one as I pass, curious if the connection is still alive, but when nothing happens, remove my hand and continue on to Zeus's house. The house feels more peaceful now than I remember it from the night Jackson came here to help Mami, as though the house itself knows that Zeus is away and it too can relax.

I reach the front door and hesitate, suddenly hyperaware that I'm about to go into Zeus's home, the very one responsible for all my troubles here—the very one I am planning to kill. I lift my fist to knock, when the door swings open and Mami stands before me. "Come in, child. The rest have not arrived, but please, come in." She holds the door for me.

I'm not sure what I expected the inside of Zeus's home to

look like. Cold. Scary. Stuffed humans on the wall. But I never expected it to feel so…familiar.

The front door leads to a wide foyer with tile and stone flooring that meet to create flower-like images that alternate in a pattern. A giant crystal chandelier hangs above our heads, so large and ornate and beautiful it made the one in the Cartier house look like a composite. The walls are empty here except for a single painting on the right wall of Zeus himself, likely there to remind anyone who enters that he is watching.

"This way," Mami says, and she continues on through the house into a two-story room that I imagine must be a sitting room or family room, though nothing about it has a "family" feel. A fire crackles from a fireplace on the left wall, in front of it a sofa and two chairs, each of them entirely too formal to be in a home.

Mami sits in one of the chairs and motions for me to sit. My eyes drop down to the table in front of the sofa. It is hand carved, the top of it the scene from a war. Soldiers are on the ground, clearly injured or dead, and to the far right corner on top of a hill is a single man, his hands outstretched as though he has harnessed all the power in the world. I wonder if Vill made Zeus this table, and if so, how he managed it without making a comment. The whole thing oozes Zeus's arrogance.

"You are opinionated, indeed," Mami says with a smile. "I can see why you bother him."

My eyes snap up from the table to find her studying me. "He bothers me, too."

She laughs. "Yes, but he bothers most. You on the other hand…" She moves from the chair to the sofa, her movements so fluid I barely process that she's in motion before she's beside me, my hand in hers. "You have a strong spirit. Determined. So brave. How did you become this way? What did they do to you to evoke it?"

I tilt my head in confusion. "Sorry? Do to me? They didn't do anything. And I'm not sure I'm brave. I do what I have to do."

"You do what is necessary to protect others. I have yet to see you act out in a selfish manner at all. Surely you can appreciate the bravery in that."

I swallow hard. She doesn't know what I know—I am selfish. I act as much because it gives me a sense of purpose as any other reason. I act to prove, even now a million light years away, that I am worthy to my father. I may come across as selfless, but really, I am one of the most selfish people I know.

Mami grips my hand a bit tighter. "Well, that may be true, but if more possessed your selfish tendencies then we may not be in this war in the first place. If others thought of the good of the whole instead of the individual, as you do. You make tough decisions, Ari. You are very special. I'm sure your father is very proud."

Tears spring to my eyes at her words and I have to look away to keep them from falling. "Jackson is special, too," I say, hoping to get the attention off me.

She smiles, clearly thinking something she refuses to say. "Very special. Come with me."

"Why did you ask if they did something to me?" I ask as we make our way further into the house and down a small hallway with photos hanging in perfect order across the wall. I stop short at the first set of photos—all of them of a small boy with white blond hair and a smile I would recognize anywhere. Jackson, even then, held a mystery in his eyes, as though he protected important information.

Mami comes up beside me, reaching out a hand to caress a photo of Jackson at the top of a cliff overlooking a waterfall. I know the spot instantly—I dreamt of this place a long time ago when Jackson first revealed himself to me.

"I know this place…" I say.

Mami just nods. "We believe in the power of words. When words are meditated on and infused into our bodies they can become a part of us."

My gaze lifts from the photo to Mami. "What do you mean infused into your bodies?"

"Jackson has never shown you?" she asks, but at my confused expression she clears her throat and focuses back on the photo. "This was taken…"

For once I'm the one to grasp her hand. "Mami, what is it? What are you saying?"

"Please…ask Jackson. It isn't fair for me to divulge what he may want kept private."

"If something has happened to him…"

She releases a long breath, hesitating. "If an RES lacks speed, as part of his training he will receive a cipher of the word *velocity* and be told to meditate on the word, feeling it sink into his skin and muscles and bones until his body listens, the cipher acting as an injection into his spirit until he is as agile as the wind itself."

"A cipher? Like a tattoo?"

"We believe every part of our body possesses recollection abilities, and when told to do something, it can and will listen. By placing the word on our skin we are telling our bodies we need whatever the word represents." She pushes up her left arm sleeve to reveal a tiny symbol in the crook of her arm. A single vertical line with three horizontal lines running through the top of it, each parallel to one another.

"What does it mean?"

"Strength."

I glance up at her, my heart heavy. What must life be like daily for Mami? Always on edge, always trying to survive. Never able to show who she truly is or how she truly feels.

My eyes drift back to the cipher, and then my mind shifts to Jackson after his trainings with Zeus, everything Mami is saying becoming clear. The blood on his shirt. His unwillingness to change in front of me. He must have received a cipher at each of his trainings, but there was so much blood. A tiny symbol like Mami's would never produce that much blood, so he must have received more than one, more than ten, more than—

I remember his blood-soaked shirt and have to take a step back to steady myself. "What has Zeus done to him?" My words are filled with every ounce of hate I have for Zeus.

Mami's eyes drop from the photo of Jackson as a boy. "I never wanted this life for him."

Then before I can respond, Emmy and Lydian walk up, their expressions filled with worry. "He knows," Lydian says. "The port is completely surrounded. I don't think we can use it to escape."

"Zeus always knows," Mami says. "But he underestimates us."

Emmy tilts her head at Mami, and then, reading her thoughts, smiles. "I forgot. Do you think he forgot, too?"

"There is only one way to be sure."

We are well into the woods behind Zeus and Mami's house before I can fully process what I've agreed to. The Earthly port is guarded, and while we could fight the RESs, something tells me that's exactly what Zeus wants. He knows we're up to something. We all agreed that for now it's better to remain low, to appear defeated, which is how we have ended up in the woods, on our way to plan B. For the first time, I'm stepping outside the Healer's Wall.

"Our mother was never a fan of the Castellos," Mami says. "So much so that when I agreed to marry Zeus, she vowed to create an exit for me, whenever I should need it. A place I could go to disappear. She wanted to keep me safe. She was an advanced healer, her talent far greater than any other. Still to this date, there has been no one to match her."

Emmy grips my hand. "She who taught me that any can heal, not just those born to it."

Mami nods. "Emmy and I were both taught well, though of course Emmy's skills have always far surpassed my own." Mami smiles over at her sister. "Before she passed, mother took us to a special tree."

"Wait," I say, stopping so suddenly the others glance around nervously. "Did you say a special tree?"

Mami's expression creases with worry. "Yes, why?"

"Jackson took me to a special tree. But it's not here, it's on Earth, in Sydia. He called it the Unity tree."

Emmy laughs. "We should've guessed he knew, Mami."

Mami is silent for several seconds, bringing the eeriness of the woods into full focus. There are no insect or animal sounds here like there are back home, and while you might think owls are creepy, take them away and suddenly the forest feels less like an open place and more like a contained room, where any noise you make is amplified. Even my breaths, so controlled, sound far too loud. "What aren't you saying, Mami?"

"I'm wondering if Zeus knew about the tree after all, or at least guessed that it existed, even if he couldn't find it. I'm sure Jackson told you that only those who know of its location can find it. Mother blessed it with an unusual heal. It exists, yet doesn't, traveling in between the dimensions so that it can appear when needed…and disappear when not. Jackson must have followed me to it at some point. He must have watched me summon it."

"But if your mother created the Unity tree as an escape for you, why would she place it beyond the wall?"

Emmy grins over at me. "Ah, you make assumptions, child. The wall has not always been."

"What?" I glance from Emmy to Mami, but it's Lydian who answers me.

"Triad was not always encaged by the wall," Lydian says. "There was a time when Loge was comprised of many regions, each with its own leader. As you can imagine, disagreements erupted, arguments became wars, and Zeus, having convinced himself the other regions were corrupted, made it his mission to lead more than just Triad—he wanted to control all of Loge. And he succeeded, but not before gaining a wealth of enemies. He claimed the wall was built to protect Triad from threats, when really it was built to protect him from his enemies. Now, his enemies are long gone and the wall is used to control the health of our land."

"But there are still other regions, right? What happened to those leaders?"

Lydian's face turns to stone. "They were handled, as all are handled who get in Zeus's way."

We walk the rest of the way through the woods in silence, each of us consumed by our own thoughts and worries. I realize that Mami may be the bravest person I've ever met. Not just anyone would have the strength to plot against her spouse, especially when that spouse is Zeus. Whatever horror would lie in store for the rest of us if we were caught would be nothing compared to what he would do to Mami. I feel a sudden pang of guilt for keeping this from Jackson. He would never want her this involved.

Mami drapes her arm around me, hugging me gently. "You have a kind spirit, child. Never let that leave you. War can harden us. I know, I've suffered through too many to count. But I like to think I was once like you—full of kindness and bravery."

"Mami, you are—"

"Look, we're here," she says before I can continue. I swallow back my guilt, knowing there is no time for that now.

It's long past time for second-guessing my actions. I have to push forward.

In front of me is the same vine-covered wall that exists in the garden by the Panacea and beyond the fields where we train, the same wall Jackson forced us to walk on our first day of RES assignee training. I'm about to ask how we can get past the wall, when I notice a tiny latch tucked into the greenery. I edge closer, reaching out to move the flowers and vegetation away, and discover that cut within the wall is a gate, barely noticeable to the naked eye. A small lock secures the latch closed, no doubt to keep out anyone who may try to enter.

I peer over my shoulder at Mami. "Do you have the key?"

Emmy laughs. "*We* are key." And she reaches out a shaking hand to the lock. Her fingertips brush over the key opening, first her thumb, then each of her fingers beginning with her index finger and ending with her pinky. A tingly feeling crawls my spine and I know regardless of how brave Mami thinks I am, I'm afraid. I'm afraid of what lies beyond the wall, of what Ancients may have survived there and what they are prepared to do with us—or to us. Then a deeper fear appears in my mind and I have to force myself not to take a step backward.

What if we die the moment we cross through the gate, our bodies becoming as lifeless as the land there?

"Dramatics. Always dramatics, child." Emmy pushes the gate open and steps through, disappearing into the darkness on the other side. A crisp breeze flows through the gate, sweeping my hair across my face. Lydian and Mami follow, and I'm left alone before the wall, no choice but to push aside my doubts and trust—something more difficult for me to do than anything else in the world. But again, there is no time for second-guessing, no time for doubts, no time for fear. There is no time for anything but action.

I repeat the words again and again in my mind until I feel strong. I draw a long breath, clench my fists tightly together, and step through the gate and into a void.

CHAPTER 25

It's as though color no longer exists. Energy. Happiness. Life. All of it a figment of the imagination, unable to surface. Everything about this place is lost, the ground nothing more than dirt so gray it's closer to ash.

I peer around in search of the others, and that's when I see it—the Unity tree, its size so much more impressive with nothing else there to compete for attention. I remember the first time Jackson brought me to it thinking it as twice the size of a normal tree, but now, seeing it again after so long, I realize I underestimated it. This tree can't be compared to other trees at all. And it's more than just its size. The Unity tree is enchanting…and haunting at the same time.

The tree itself radiates life, making it appear all that more beautiful in this dead land. The leaves are so shiny and green they remind me of the tiny leaves on the composite holly bushes back home. The bark, the limbs, even the tiny twigs that are of no use, all appear perfectly fake compared to the trees within the wall. It's almost like staring at a miracle, but then my eyes drop to the triangular opening in the center, so dark it's as though part of the tree has been burned…or cursed. "How is possible that Zeus doesn't know this is here?" I ask, unwilling to take my eyes away from the dark center.

Mami places her palm against the bark and smiles. "Oh he suspects, he just can't see it. Mother made sure of that."

"And where does it take you? If we went inside the opening now, where would we end up?"

Mami turns to me. "Wherever you tell it to take you. It is not connected to a direct port on Earth like the other trees, though it utilizes the same principle. If you concentrate on Sydia, you will end up in Sydia."

Frustration bubbles in my chest at her carefree demeanor. She acts as though we are on a casual outing, as though the survival of both species isn't counting on us. "I need details, Mami. Will we end up in the center of the city or in the woods? Does it connect to a tree? A interplanetary port? I can't leave this stuff to chance. I need to know exactly where it will take us, how it works. Everyone is counting on us and time is running out."

Emmy reaches for my hand, but I pull away. "Calm, child. Mami know. We all know."

I scrub my hands over my face, realizing my own worry and doubts are causing me to lash out. As much as I wish none of this were happening, I'm ready to get started. Sitting around aimlessly, while the clock ticks toward the war, has me on edge. We can plan. We can scheme. But at the end of the day I have a feeling none of that will matter. Our success hinges on two things—luck and whether or not I succeed in killing Zeus.

Mami drapes her arm around me, making me feel even guiltier for getting aggravated at her. "All ports are direct links, it's not an unknown. You can't enter a tree and end up in open space. It has to tie to a specific thing, even if that specific thing is your choice. The woods that border Sydia are the perfect place."

"Okay. The woods, then. We will have three landing sites, that way if one group is caught the other two are still safe and can offer help."

"Very smart thinking," she says, squeezing me easily. "You will make an amazing commander some day."

I clear my throat and look away. "I think that day is long past."

Mami turns to me, her eyes gentle. "You are not going into the end, child. Trust that. This is the beginning, and what the beginning looks like is in your hands, no one else's."

I pray she's right, that in a few years this is all a memory, but inside I've prepared myself that I may not make it through this—none of us may.

···

I left the others at Mami's, telling them I needed to get home to meet with Cybil, and while I am meeting her in another hour, for now I just want to be alone. I've thought through every element of this plan. The two divisions—Operatives and RES assignees. What they will do and when. Everyone knows where to be, at what time, and what to do once they get there. Even with the original port guarded, we are still on track thanks to the Unity tree. Everything is set to begin at one a.m. in two days, all of it planned to the smallest detail.

All except how I'm going to kill Zeus.

I enter our house, glad that it's quiet, and head immediately down to Jackson's office, hopeful that somehow the connection is back. I want to talk to my dad. I want his advice. I want him, and no one else, to tell me that I can do this—that I will do this. Because if I hear the words from him, then I will know it's true.

Dad was never one to coddle. He would never tell me that I would succeed unless it was true. And so now, days before I'm about to do the scariest thing imaginable—go up against Zeus—I want my dad's reassurance, something so childish that I'm almost embarrassed to admit it to myself.

Still, I remind myself of Mom's lecture to me years ago when Dad first told me that I would become an Operative. I was afraid, and even though I would never admit it out loud, she knew. So that night, long after Dad had gone to bed, she came into my room and sat down on my bed, her face the picture of ease. "Fear is what makes us human, Ari," she had said. "It grounds us, helps us make smarter decisions. Never feel inadequate for feeling fear. It's the most natural thing in the world, and knowing that it is natural is what will give you the strength to overcome it."

Sitting down in front of the communicator screen, I draw a breath and close my eyes, the memory so clear in my mind I can almost smell my mom's perfume. I press my palm to the screen. "Dad?" My eyes flicker open, hopeful, but the screen remains dark, so I shut my eyes and pretend he can hear me. "Dad, if you're there, if you can hear me, I want you to know that I finally understand why you pushed me so hard. I thought you did it to try to make me as strong and capable as you, when really you pushed me because you knew this day was coming. You knew I would have to fight in a real war where there are no guarantees of survival. You prepared me well, Dad. I only wish you were here to fight alongside me. Then I would know that I could do it."

My lip trembles, and I have to swallow several times to keep myself from breaking down. I picture my dad in front of me. His strength. His courage. "Because with you beside me, there is nothing I couldn't do. Tell Mom I love her." I swipe away a lone tear that escaped, and start to stand, when the door bursts open.

"They're back!" Cybil screams. "They're back and we're not set up, we're not ready. We're not ready for this. We need another day. We—"

"What? Who—oh no."

Cybil nods, her face full of panic. "Zeus is back a day early. The plan, it's—"

I raise my hands, cutting her off, and glance back at the time. Eight o'clock. Dad used to say that you could plan an attack, but you could never plan for what would go wrong in your planning, so be ready. And we're ready, I know it deep in my gut. We have only five hours until the RESs switch shifts, but that's enough. It has to be enough. "Get the word out to the others. We attack tonight."

"Ari…"

"We have no other option."

"What about Zeus?"

"I'll handle Zeus. Just get the others to Earth They're counting on us, Cybil. We can't let them down."

Cybil surprises me with a hug, holding me tightly as though she may never see me again. "Are the healers rubbing off on you or something?" I laugh to try to lighten the mood, but I know without needing to read her thoughts that we're thinking the same thing—a lot of lives are about to be lost and there is no way of knowing who will make it through. Including us.

"Just make it to the tree, okay?"

I smile. "The next time I see you we'll be in Sydia."

CHAPTER 26

When Jackson arrives home an hour later, I'm in the backyard, surrounded by dead grass. I devised my plan against Zeus the moment Cybil left, deciding that it'd be best to keep it to myself. I can't risk someone accidentally revealing the plan to him. Even Cybil, who I trust completely. I have a hard enough time controlling my thoughts around Zeus. Plus, if no one else knows the plan, then no one else can be tortured for information. This is between Zeus and me. Besides…what I'm planning has never been done before, and the last thing I need right now is a look of doubt from Cybil. My own doubts are enough.

Lydian's brew should have weakened Zeus's reflexes by now. So my plan is to reverse heal him, pulling the life out of him like Vill and Emmy had said, just as the Ancient attackers were able to Take the life from their victims back on Earth. I can't utilize the Taking. It can't be used from Ancient to Ancient, a biological failsafe to protect the species from each other. But if our minds are strong enough to give life then I have to believe they are strong enough to take it. I close my eyes and focus on the next patch of grass in front of me. I feel its life, its energy, and then instead of strengthening that life, I imagine it moving from the grass into me. I focus all my senses, all thought, every single part of my body and soul into pulling the life from the grass. When I open my eyes, the patch of grass is shriveled and brown, and my skin is tingling.

"So…are you going to tell me what you're doing? Are you all right?" Jackson asks from behind me. I wonder how long he's been there—how much he's seen. I stand up and turn around slowly, preparing what I'll say in my mind, when my eyes land on his, so full of concern for me that it takes my breath away. "I…" My words get jumbled in my mind. All I can think about is how this may be the last time we're together, the last time I can…

I rush forward, wrap my arms around his neck, and, taking one last fleeting look at his face, allow my lips to find his, desperate to soak in every ounce of him. I let his scent, his touch, his everything, overcome me, all of it enough to make me wish I could lose myself in this moment and never wake up. I grip the bottom of his T-shirt, eager to pull him closer, but instead of the feel of soft cotton, his shirt feels cold, damp.

"Jackson, what…?" I bring my hands around so I can see them and gasp. They are covered in blood.

I race around to the back of him, preparing to lift his shirt, when he grabs my wrists, holding me at a distance. "What are you doing?"

My eyes flash with anger. "What happened to you?"

He looks away. "Nothing. It's nothing."

"It's not nothing. Look at my hands, Jackson. That isn't nothing—that's blood. *Your* blood. Show me your back."

He laughs uncomfortably. "Minutes home and already you're trying to take my clothes off."

"This isn't funny. Let me see it."

He takes a step away from me, keeping his back away from view. "See what? You're acting crazy."

"The cipher. Let me see the cipher."

As soon as the word leaves my lips, Jackson's entire demeanor changes. "How do you know about ciphers?"

"Mami told me. And that doesn't matter. Let me see yours."

His face morphs from fear to anger. "When did you see Mami?"

Suddenly my words feel reckless. It should have been Mami to tell him, not me. "Jackson…"

"Why have you seen her?"

"It's…she's…"

"Just tell me!"

"She's helping, okay? She came to see me. She wanted to help. I didn't—"

Jackson advances toward me. "Do you have any idea what you've done involving her? He would hurt her just for talking to you. If he finds out she's helping you, he'll…" He rakes his fingers through his hair and turns away from me. "I should never have… This can't be happening."

Now that his back is to me, I can see the damage to his shirt in plain view. The blood starts with a large blob at the top left around his shoulder and trickles down in a red river to the bottom of his shirt, where it meets another large blob. I reach out for his back, touching the top blob easily. "What has he done to you?"

Jackson whips around quickly, taking another step away from me. "I don't have time for this. I'm grabbing a shower and then you're going to tell me everything. Understand?"

"Jackson—"

"No. There is nothing right about this. Nothing." And he turns for the shower before I can say another word. The water starts up and for a moment I consider going in the house, but that was the old Ari. In less than five hours we're starting a rebellion. I've lost communication with Earth. And on top of all that, I have to right my mind with the fact that I am going up against the most powerful Ancient in existence. I understand that Jackson is angry, he has a right to be angry, but we don't have time for anger, not when we have no guarantees that we can say we're sorry later.

And it's with that in mind that I step into the shower, fully clothed, shutting the door and blocking it, so he can't escape. I draw a shaky breath, forcing my eyes to stay on his face.

"Are you insane?" Jackson shouts, making sure to keep his back against the shower wall.

I inch closer, my hands out like I'm trying to calm a wild animal. "Look, I refuse to fight. Not now. Not ever. I'm sorry I didn't tell you about Mami. She asked me not to, likely to keep you protected. She loves you so much." I drop my gaze for just a second. "*I* love you so much. Which is why it hurts me to see you hurt. It hurts me to know that he's hurting you and there's nothing I can do to stop it. You won't even let me see it. I just… Please…let me help you."

"You can't help me," he whispers.

I am to him now, and if before I thought I knew pain, it was nothing compared to this. Jackson's face shows all the horror that I know he's endured. He looks like a lost child, the pain on his face so intense it makes my insides ache. I place my hands on his arms, and I can tell he's trying hard to stay strong. "Actually…I can. I should have told you this sooner. I don't know why I didn't. I just…"

"What are you saying?"

My eyes meet his. "I can heal."

"What do you mean?"

"Emmy taught me. I'm nowhere near as good as her or the other healers. But if you'll let me, I can show you, I can try." I start to turn him around, nodding reassurance when he hesitates. And then Jackson's back is to me and I want to cry,

I want to scream, I want to stab Zeus in the chest and watch with joy as he slowly bleeds to death. Because every visible bit of skin, every inch, is covered in markings, some put in so deeply they look more like scars than tattoos. There are too many to count, many crossing over each other so his back is more green than the tan of his skin. I swallow hard, my eyes lifting to his left shoulder where a fresh cipher bleeds down his back.

"Why isn't xylem healing it?" I ask as I move my fingers easily around the wound.

Jackson flinches as I touch the edge of the cipher, which looks like a sun with a dagger through it. "Ciphering is an old form of medicine. For a cipher to work, it has to heal on its own, once the skill or virtue becomes a part of us. Originally, they were used to gauge when the sickness they were intended to medicate no longer ailed the patient. Now, I think Zeus just enjoys knowing that we're suffering in the name of greatness. A healer can…"

I close my eyes and rest my palm over the cipher, feeling its energy, feeling the pain it inflicts. I concentrate on each of its lines, the smooth curve of the sun, the jagged edges of the dagger. I let it pierce my mind through and through until it feels as though the cipher is a tangible thing within me that I can control, move—erase. I open my eyes and lift my palm from his back, a triumphant smile on my face. "Heal?"

Jackson peeks over his left shoulder, to where the cipher used to be. "How did you do that?" He starts to turn back, but I stop him so I can heal the four other ciphers on his back, each either scabbed or still bleeding.

"How many do you have?" I ask as I trace my fingertip over a tiny one in the center of his back that looks like an eye.

Goose bumps rise on his skin as the eye begins to disappear. "I stopped counting when I received my fiftieth."

"Fifty? How are there even fifty skills or virtues worth having?"

"Some are duplicates. I guess Zeus felt those skills were especially lacking." He shrugs as though it doesn't matter to him, but I hear the hurt in his voice. Regardless of what he says, he wants Zeus's approval.

I trace a darkened heart under his right shoulder blade, breathing in and out easily, no longer needing to close my eyes to heal him. Just seeing the wound is enough. "I'm sorry he's done this to you." I make my way to the small of his back where a large compass bleeds down over his backside. My eyes drop to the tight contours, and I have to remind myself to keep breathing.

Jackson turns around so he's facing me. "This, what you did, it's amazing. You're amazing."

"No, I'm not. I'm reckless and prideful and selfish. And I'm scared, Jackson. I'm so scared." I feel tears welling in my eyes and for the first time I don't try to blink them away. "I should be focused and ready. I should be brave. But I'm not. I'm afraid of so many things right now that I can hardly breathe. I…" I swallow back a sob, knowing if I allow myself to break down now I'll never get the strength back to do what I have to do.

"Shh…" Jackson brushes my soaked hair back and places his hands on either side of my face. "There's a reason why everyone comes to you, Ari. Why Emmy came to you. Why Mami came to you. We know that you can succeed where others have failed. So you may be afraid, and that's okay, but you should know that the rest of us aren't and it's because of you."

My lip trembles. "But what if I can't—"

"You will."

"But it's Zeus. He's—"

"You will, Ari. You will."

I raise my eyes. "What if I fail?"

"You won't."

And as though his words are a spark, igniting my body, my lips crash into his, each touch and caress and kiss slowly taking away my fear. I know I have things to do, plans to make, but for now I want this moment. After all, there are no guarantees that I will ever get it again.

Jackson slips his hands under my wet shirt, pulling me closer to him, deepening the kiss, before moving down my neck. He pushes the edge of my shirt off my shoulder and continues his trail over my collarbone, his lips warm, his touch soft. I release a small moan as his hand cups one of my breasts, and with it, all thought is gone, replaced by passion.

Jackson yanks my shirt over my head and lifts me up so my legs wrap tightly around him. He edges to the wall of the shower and takes turns kissing my lips, then my neck, then my breasts, and back until I'm sure I'm going to explode.

He sets me down gently and pulls away, as though to ask permission, but the words never leave his lips. Instead, he slides his hands down the curve of my waist and grips my hips. His eyes drop to my pants and then back to my face and then before doubt can seep into either of our minds, he unbuttons them and slides them down, pulling me to him again, now nothing between us, just skin against skin, and I know that this moment will remain etched into my mind for the rest of my life. I love him with such an intense need that for the first time in my life, I feel whole, I feel right, I feel as though every flaw I have is now erased, filled by him. He is my perfect opposite, and now I know I don't have to do this on my own. I can lean on him, and he can lean on me, and together we can succeed. Not alone. But together.

Jackson turns the shower off and we towel each other dry, our eyes unable to leave each other's. I rise onto my toes and kiss his lips, then his cheeks and eyes. I feel as though I could stay here forever, kissing every inch of his beautiful skin, but the time for me is gone, and now I have to give myself over to my mission.

It's time for final planning. Time to kill Zeus.

CHAPTER 27

I take my time getting dressed while Jackson grabs us some vitamin tonic from the kitchen. I dress in all black, fitted clothes, making sure that I can move easily in them. I have no idea what going up against Zeus will entail, but I'm not ruling out combat fighting and something tells me Zeus is much tougher than his age would suggest.

I run through potential scenarios as I open the weapons drawer in our closet, torn between using the gun Jackson gave me originally, the RES gun, or choosing something else entirely. Various knives and guns shine brightly back at me, all eager to be used. I grab a small knife from the stash, pulling it from its sheath. It's nothing special, a standard six-inch fixed blade, one side razor sharp, the other serrated. I strap it to my right leg and walk around, checking to make sure I can still move easily. Satisfied, I return to the drawer and select one of the force field guns I saw the RESs training with a few weeks ago. With Zeus, immobilizing him will be key.

I slide the gun into my left boot and test my ability to move again. All feels good, so I start for the door, and then hesitating, choose another gun just in case. Dad always said you can't have too many guns, and if nothing else, at root I am my father's daughter through and through.

Feeling confident with my selections, I peek around at the clock. Ten thirty. Jackson went to get the tonics nearly thirty minutes ago. Worry slices through my insides, and I'm out the door, running through the hall. "Jackson? Jackson, where are you?" The common room is empty, the kitchen dark. There are no sounds through the house, no hints at all that he's there somewhere, doing something and just lost track of time. I make my way into the kitchen, unsure of what else to do, and freeze. The kitchen looks completely untouched, except for two cups on the countertop, one knocked on its side, its orange contents still dripping to the floor. I feel my chest constrict, my lungs unwilling to suck in a breath. "Jackson…please," I call, but I know he won't answer. He's gone, and only one person could have done this.

He knows. Knows all of it maybe. Which means Jackson isn't just gone, he's being used as bait.

The thought sends my body into turbo mode. I head back to the weapons' drawer and shove another couple of knives and a gun into my boots and pants, anywhere I can think to hide one. Forget going in stealth-like. This changes everything.

I run into Vill on my way out, my mind so focused that I don't hear him calling my name until I'm halfway down the front steps.

"Ari, what's wrong? What happened?" he asks as I turn.

"They have Jackson."

"Who?"

"Zeus. He took Jackson."

"I don't understand."

I sigh loudly. "Look, I don't have time to explain. Zeus took Jackson. We have mere hours before the plan starts. And I have to somehow find Jackson, release him from whatever hold he's under, and kill Zeus. So as I was saying, I don't have time for this." I set off down the street, Vill now on my heels.

"Wait, you can't just—Ari, wait. I can help." He grabs my arm to stop me and I wiggle free, growing more frustrated by the second.

"You know Zeus, Vill. You know what he's capable of. I gave the order to start our evacuation plan already. Everything is in motion. We only have a few hours to get Jackson out of there. Do you understand what I'm telling you? I don't have time to create a new plan. There's only time for action." I start back for the bridge, when I feel his arm on me again. "Don't make me hurt you. I don't want that, but I will if you try to stand in my way."

"I know where Zeus likely took him. I can help if you'll let me."

I stop, seeing for the first time just how worried he is over his cousin. "Okay, talk then. But you'll have to talk as we walk. You think he's in the Castello building?"

Vill keeps pace beside me. "Yes. I'm guessing in one of the holding cells in the basement. They aren't used anymore, but they were built to question captives back when Zeus was waging war against the other regions. There's a back entrance."

"Good thinking."

"Yeah, what were you going to do? Walk through the main entrance, point a gun, and demand Jackson? I'm sure that would have worked perfectly."

I don't look over. "Honestly, I haven't given a lot of thought to how I'm going to get him. All I know is that I have to. There's no telling what Zeus will do to him." I swallow hard to keep my thoughts in check. I don't want to think of what horrors Jackson is enduring right this second, all because of me. He won't kill him, but death would be merciful compared to what Zeus might do.

I pick up my speed. "Do you think Zeus is with him?"

"Oh you can count on it."

"Good."

We slow down as we reach the Castello building and edge around to the back, though I'm sure Zeus already knows we're there. Vill holds the back door for me and we go down a set of stairs that remind me of Jackson and my break into Parliament headquarters. It feels like years ago since we were there. I remember thinking that everything was so complicated, so intense. That day was a chocolate covered rainbow compared to what I'm walking into.

The basement level of the building has the same look and feel as the Vortex, all gray and business. Vill points down the long hallway in front of us, ignoring the six doors on the right and left along the way. "At the end of the hall is a containment room. It was once used to get information out of hostages."

"And you think Jackson's there?" I ask, lowering my voice, though I'm not sure why. If Zeus can see us, he can also hear us.

"One way to find out." Vill is at the end of the hall before I realize it's a setup. I call out for Vill just as the containment door opens and a guard exits, knocking Vill out with the butt of his gun. Another guard steps out and then Zeus appears from the shadows.

"Would you believe he said you wouldn't come?" Zeus says, his hands behind him as he walks slowly toward me. "I assured him your love was stronger than that, but he claimed you wouldn't be so foolish. He is too young yet to realize that love is tantamount to fool." His head jerks. "T-tantamount: equivalent in seriousness to, virtually the same."

"You're insane."

He smiles. "Greatness often mingles with insanity. They are, after all, old friends."

"Where is he? What have you done with him?"

The smile deepens into an evil grin. "In time." He continues forward as I reach behind me for the guns strapped to my back. "Admirable, but I wouldn't do that if I were you." He looks over my shoulder and I turn to see two more guards closing in on me. "See, I knew they would at some point ask you to kill me. Honestly, I'm surprised they had to ask. But what fun would it be to simply watch you try? I had to give you a reason to succeed. Hence, my grandson. Nothing ignites the passion to kill like threatening someone we love, wouldn't you agree?"

"How would you know? Like you've ever loved anyone in your life." I glance between the two guards, the intensity of the situation causing my senses to heighten. And then the decision is made before I've consciously accepted it, and I'm in motion, to Zeus before he can respond, whipping a knife from my boot, securing him from behind, and placing the knife to his neck. The guards all start forward. "Make a move and this knife finds its home in his throat."

"I find it humorous that you feel you have the control here."

"Well, I am the one with a knife to your throat."

Zeus laughs, causing the knife to slice into his skin. "Very well, bring her out," he says. I shake my head in confusion, assuming he's talking to me, when the middle right door opens and another guard steps out, this one with a gun to Mami's head.

I gasp, torn between keeping my position and rushing to save her. A million thoughts zoom through my head all at once—How did this happen? Did someone betray us? Who else does he have?—and then I realize I'm ticking toward a mental breakdown and force myself to draw a long steadying breath. I focus in on the gun, on the guard, and start to close my eyes when Mami speaks, her voice as calm as a spring breeze, "No. Focus on him, not me. He won't kill me." Her gaze falls on Zeus, equal parts disappointment and rage. "Will you, love?

You're too afraid to be alone. That's why you keep your guards so close. Deep down you're afraid."

"Do you believe her words, Ari?" Zeus says, his voice taking on the manic tone I've heard from him when he's at his craziest.

"Mami…"

"And do you want to know who he fears most?" she asks. "You. Because he knows you're the one who is going to destroy him."

My eyes dart to the guard, poised to shoot. What is Mami doing? She's going to get herself killed! "Mami—" I stop at the look on her face. Oh no. *No*, I think, hoping she can hear me. *You can't do this. Don't.*

Sirens sound from outside, and I know they've intercepted our escape route, that the fight has begun. I have to get to Jackson. Time is running out. *Mami, please…*

Get to Jackson. He's locked in Zeus's office. I'm counting on you. He's the only thing in the world that matters to me. Her gaze turns soft. *I'm so thankful he found you.* Then she closes her eyes and the lights flash in the hall. The guard yells out in pain. "Stay strong, child," Mami says. Zeus opens his mouth, but I'll never know what he was going to say. A shot rings through the hall, Mami's eyes widen, and then her body slumps to the floor.

"No!" Zeus screams, and in one quick movement, he's out of my hold and to the guard, snapping his neck as though it's nothing but a twig. He collapses on his knees beside Mami, his head jerking in shock. "Can't. No. This—no, Mami, no." I think he's going to break into sobs, when he leaps up and starts for me, his eyes on fire. "You did this."

"No. You have tortured her every day of her life with you. Don't get remorseful now. *You* did this." My lip shakes as I glance back at her limp body. "You killed her. And now I'm going to kill you." I focus my gaze on him, listening to the drum of his heart, the gentle whooshing of his breath. I follow the sounds to the organs that create them, and then with a single blink of the eye, I lock in on them, sucking the life from each faster than xylem can heal them. Zeus bucks forward onto his hands and knees from the shock of it. I walk toward him, never feeling so satisfied in all my life. Finally, this monster who has created so much turmoil will be gone, and we can all live peacefully on Earth.

"Is that what you think?" he manages to wheeze out. "There is…no…such thing…as peace." He falls sideways and I stand over him, torn between watching him die and getting to Jackson quickly.

And that moment of hesitation is what gives Zeus his single chance to strike. He pulls a knife from his pants and shoves it into my calf. I cry out, releasing my mental hold on him, and he leaps up, tossing me hard to the ground and reaching back to stab me again. I block his arm just as the knife is about to pierce my chest, grunting with the effort of holding him back.

Like Emmy, he has strength far greater than expected of his age and after several seconds of holding him, I feel my muscles wavering and the knife dips closer to my chest. I close my eyes, trying to find something, anything in me, to use against him, but the effort of holding him back has zapped all my focus.

"Oh how nice it will be to watch you die," Zeus says, and then suddenly he screams out in pain. He falls away from me into a ball on the ground, clawing at his head. I jump up, more afraid than I've ever been in my life, and glance around, desperate to find whoever is doing this to Zeus. And that's when I see Vill standing a few yards away, his eyes trained on Zeus, and I know he's using his mind to weaken Zeus.

"Well come on, we don't have all day," he says to me.

"I'm not leaving until I know he's dead." I start forward, just as two more guards round the corner, their weapons drawn.

"Freeze. Weapons down!" they scream.

Vill tries to maintain his focus on Zeus, but each second Zeus grows stronger, pushing away Vill's power over him. I eye the guards and then Zeus, knowing I have only seconds. I rip the gun from my left boot and fire twice at the guards, just as one shoots. I race forward, not stopping to make sure the guards are down, not stopping to make sure Vill is okay, all thought, all my energy on Zeus. I reach him, just as he leaps up, his knife raised.

"What now, Ari dear?"

He lunges forward just as a shot rings out through the halls. His body freezes midmotion, shock envelops his face, and then a blot of blood spreads across his shirt. I glance around frantically and see Mami's head raised, a gun in her hand. She must have pulled it from the guard who shot her. I rush to her and her arm drops, the gun sliding across the floor.

"Mami? Are you okay? Mami?" I search for her wound, but her entire torso is covered in blood. I place a hand on her face. "I'm so sorry. I'm so sorry."

Her eyes glass over and she takes a jagged breath. "Take care of him." Then her head falls to the side.

I feel a hand touch my shoulder and I whip around, pulling a knife from my pocket. Vill raises his hands. "It's just me. We have to go."

I glance once more at Mami, my heart heavy, then stand. I walk over to Zeus and stare at his lifeless body, expecting him to snap back to life, return from the dead like one of those monsters in our storybooks back home. But he doesn't move, his chest no longer lifts and his eyes no longer flutter. Every part of him is still, and for the first time since coming to Loge, an overwhelming sense of security washes over me. I had no idea just how afraid I was of Zeus until that moment. And now that he's gone, I'm ready to go home. I'm ready to see my family and friends and to let them know that the fight is over.

Zeus is dead.

CHAPTER 28

Vill directs us through a series of hallways, to a set of stairs that leads up through the center of the building. Shots continue to go off in the distance, and in the back of my mind I wonder how many we've lost and what I could have done to better prepare them for the fight. But for now, I can't worry about that. I have to get to Jackson.

The stab wound in my leg has nearly healed, but despite xylem's healing properties, the wound still feels sensitive, like a fresh bruise. I remind myself that pain is a mental thing, that I can block it out. I have to.

We reach Zeus's office to find a pair of guards waiting, as though they knew we'd arrive at just that moment. Worry seeps through my core. Vill didn't kill the other two guards, just wounded them, so maybe they called up. That has to be it...Zeus can't be alive. Mami shot him. His body was still. But I didn't check for a pulse. Why didn't I check for a pulse?

Suddenly loud footsteps close in on us from all sides, and within seconds, we're surrounded, twelve guards to the two of us.

"This isn't good," Vill says out of the corner of his mouth.

"On the count of three, you get into the office and find Jackson. I'll hold them back here and then meet you inside."

I draw a long breath, ignoring the shouts from the guards for us to stand down, to drop our weapons before they shoot. "One, two, THREE!"

Vill races for the office door, while I fire at the guards closest to me, and take off down the hall to my left, hoping I can divert them from Vill long enough for him to find Jackson. A series of doors comes up on my right and left and I dip into the first one I see, crouching down out of view of the glass and wait until I hear the guards rush past. I can tell by the footsteps that not all of them followed, but hopefully enough did that I can handle the ones remaining by Zeus's door.

I peek out the glass to make sure the hall is clear and edge out of the room and back down the hall the way I came toward Zeus's office. Glancing around the corner, I can see two guards remaining, but know there could be others out of view. Regardless, I have to get inside that office.

I duck my head to ready myself for what I'm about to do. If there are more than four guards out there, I'm likely going to get shot. I close my eyes and try to sense them, their emotions, something, but feel nothing. They must be trained to control them in a fight situation.

I pull a second gun and swing out from behind the wall, both guns raised. As expected, there are two others waiting for me, both firing the moment I appear. I shoot quickly, racing for the door, and slip through just as a bullet grazes my arm. I scramble up and lock the door, spinning around with both guns poised to shoot, but the office is empty. The guards try to get through the door to no avail, so feeling safe from that side, I edge forward, my eyes alert for any movement. Being this close to the window, I can hear almost constant firing, much more than expected, which means some of the Ancients have joined in the fight. They've rebelled. All I can hope is that more are with us than against us.

There are four doors in Zeus's office, one being the one I just locked, so that leaves three to check. I reach the first on the left, gently turning the knob, then jerk it open, gun extended. A closet. An empty closet. I start for the next door, when a loud scream of pain sounds from the third. Vill.

I'm across the room in one leap and through the door before my mind can slow me down. It's a long hallway that seems to go on forever, like a secret passageway. I realize I have no idea where I'm going, so I stop and listen, hoping to hear voices or sense someone's emotions. After several seconds, I continue forward softly, not wanting to miss a sound. I'm about to round a corner, when a familiar voice calls out, "No need to hurry. He's already passed out."

I turn the corner to see Lydian over Vill's body and something comes alive within me at being betrayed so completely. Something cold, something soulless—something deadly. On some level, I have always had too much care for the enemy. I don't enjoy war, the hypocrisy of it. We send in people to fight, who then become our enemies, yet those people are just doing their jobs. We fight each other because some higher figure tells us to. It's not our fight, it's theirs, yet they are cowards in their offices, watching while we bleed each other to death.

I have watched as Parliament issued a mass killing to their people. I have watched as Zeus killed for no other reason than to show his own strength. No more. These people can fight each other if they want, but I will not stand by while another innocent—human or Ancient alike—dies in this stupid war.

I drop my head and gaze up at her, my expression lethal. "Where is Jackson?"

"He is…detained?"

I start forward, instantly feeling Lydian's strength pushing me back, but I continue on, fighting against it with a will stronger than anything I've felt before. "Where is he?"

"I told you—"

"Where is he?" I shout, firing the gun so it hits the wall, narrowly missing her head. "The next shot hits you square. That's my one and only warning. Where is he, you traitor?"

Lydian's jaw sets, and then a wave of nausea washes over me and it's all I can do to stay standing. But I do. I hold my ground, locking my feet to the spot and concentrating on my own energy, breathing into it like oxygen to a flame. I won't let her weaken me.

"You can throw everything you have at me and I won't fall. I will *never* fall." I raise my gun and shoot, hitting Lydian in the chest. Her body flies backward. Any other day I would feel a hint of guilt in my chest, something that reminds me that I'm human, but that's gone now. I'm no longer a child. They've all taken that from me, stolen it from my very soul, leaving behind some remnants of a person. I don't know what I am now—part human, part Ancient—but I do know that it doesn't matter. None of that matters. I shoot again and her body slides down the wall, leaving a trail of blood in its wake.

I kneel beside her. "The next shot is a kill shot. Tell me where he is, now."

Her body shakes as her eyes lock on mine. "He was never here, you stupid girl. All of this was a distraction. You thought you could beat Zeus. You can't." She closes her eyes and reopens them slowly.

"Zeus is dead. I watched him die."

She smirks. "Are you sure about that?"

A rush of adrenaline courses through me. Why didn't I check his pulse? Why? I press the gun to her temple. "Where is Jackson?"

Her breathing becomes labored. Xylem can heal her wounds, but it can't push out the bullet. She's slowly bleeding to death. "He's gone. Zeus took him. Don't you see? All this is for nothing. You can't beat him, Ari."

"We'll see about that." I rush over to Vill and press my palm to him, pushing some of my energy into him so he can heal. After an excruciating second he sits up, a trail of sweat on his face.

"What happened?"

"Zeus is alive. He has Jackson." I start for the door beside Lydian, hoping it leads out of the building when she says, "You won't make it. They're already gone."

I take one more look at her before firing a final bullet into her head. "Thanks for the confidence." And then I'm racing through the door, forgetting everything else—all that I've done and all I know I'm about to do. I have to find Jackson. I feel myself slipping away, each second a fraction of me rips away from my body and I know he's the only one who can keep me whole. Without him…without him, I don't know what I'll become.

Sure enough, the door leads to a private exit and within seconds, Vill and I are outside the back of the building, the gunfire so loud now it's almost deafening.

"Where should we go? Where would he have taken him?"

Vill considers for a moment, then grabs my hand. "This way. He's at the port."

I run to keep pace with Vill, who's directing us through the woods, toward the Juniper Gardens. "Why would he go to the port?"

"It's quick access to the other regions. He's either going to another region or teleporting to Earth. I can't imagine he'd go to Earth yet. He's got to be going to another region."

I pull Vill to a stop. "What if he's already gone? What then?"

Vill looks away. "Let's hope we get there in time."

We keep pace through the woods, around the factories, and slip into the Taking Forest, the fight coming into sight. There are fifty or more guards around the port, firing at random. Shots shine bright in the darkness from around the Panacea, and I realize with joy that those must be allies. We're still in the fight.

Vill leads us to the back of the port, and we're almost inside, when I hear fast footsteps approaching from behind and I turn just as someone slams me to the ground. I fight against the male guard, and then Vill fires, shooting him in the back. I roll his body off me and clamor to standing. "Thanks."

My eyes dart around, but so far no one else is advancing, so we slip inside the port. It's completely contained, no windows, and only the two doors on opposing sides. There is nothing inside, only two stone columns etched with symbols and characters, spaced at least six feet apart, and then a screen beside it with columns listing places and times.

"Is that it?" I ask.

Vill nods, concern on his face. "They've already gone, Ari. Here," he says, pointing at the screen. "Someone left two minutes ago for the Briya region. That had to be them."

"Well then let's go. We can head there too, right?"

Vill stares at the ground, his head shaking in defeat.

"Vill?"

Just then the door we came through bursts open, and Cybil, along with five others, rushes in, shutting the door hard behind them and leaning against it. "They're coming," she says.

"What about the Unity tree? What happened?" I ask.

"They knew, Ari. I got some through before they came, then circled back here to get others before they realized what we were doing. They knew everything. We have to get out of here. Now." Her expression changes. "What's wrong?"

"I can't. He has Jackson. I can't leave him, Cybil. I can't."

A pounding starts on the opposite door, and Vill and two others rush over to block it. I suck in a sharp breath, sure that any second my mind is going to crack. I glance from door to door, my eyes wide, unsure of what to do.

Cybil is to me in one long step. "Ari!" She shakes me hard. "What happened?"

I meet her gaze. "I thought I killed Zeus, but I didn't. I didn't. He's alive. And he has Jackson. We don't know if they've already gone through or haven't made it here yet. There's a time stamp for travel to Briya, but we aren't sure."

Suddenly the sound of gunfire starts to close in. I have seconds to make this decision. Seconds.

"Ari," Cybil says.

I press my palms to my face and scream into them in frustration.

"Ari!"

I glance up at her, and for the first time, realize just how lucky I have been that she was here. I might have lost myself a long time ago if not for her. "You go. Take the others through. I'll be right behind you. I just have to be sure."

"Ari, he might not even be a—"

"No. Don't say it. He's alive. I know it."

Cybil sighs heavily. "All right." She turns to the others. "I'll go in first in case we're attacked on the other side. Remember, we're going to the woods in Sydia. Follow close behind. I want someone going through every second, understand?" She pulls me into a tight hug. "See you soon?"

"Soon," I repeat. And then she crosses through the columns, disappearing immediately. The rest continue to go through, one after another, until they're all gone and it's just Vill and me, blocking both of the doors, waiting, though I already know it's futile. They're gone.

"We have to go, Ari," Vill says to me. "We have to go.

I promised him." I shake my head frantically, but before I can say a word, a force hits the door I'm standing against, knocking me forward. Vill races to me, grabs me around the waist, and yanks me through the the port, leaving everything behind.

"No!" I scream, and then a strange sensation rushes over me, beginning at my head and spiraling to my feet, over and over again, until finally I'm being tugged forward, and I fall onto my hands and knees into a bed of leaves.

Coughing hard, I scramble up to standing. "No! Jackson!" I start forward, when the sound of a gun cocking from behind me stops me cold.

"Weapons down," someone shouts. I turn slowly and feel my stomach drop. Cybil and the others are all on the ground, cuffed. Vill is unconscious beside me. And there are Operatives on all sides, all heavily armed, all preparing to shoot.

"I'm Ari Alexander," I say. "I have been working with my father, Commander Alexander, and Lawrence Cartier to take down Zeus and bring the humans home. I am not a threat. We are not a threat."

"Weapon down!" the Operative in front of me shouts again.

"You don't understand, I'm —"

"We know who you are," he says, aligning the laser on his gun with my chest.

This can't be happening. "I'm not sure who gave you your orders, but if you could just —"

"I gave the order."

My insides sour as the voice registers in my mind. Law.

Lawrence steps around the Operative, dressed in Operative gear himself. "I gave the order," he repeats. "Now drop your weapon." He pulls a gun, and I feel like I've stepped into a nightmare. Law doesn't handle guns.

This isn't right. This isn't real. It can't be. This *can't* be.

I hear the safety click off, and the world around me stops. "Law…what are you doing?"

"Drop your weapon!"

"Law—"

He fires, I feel a sharp pain in my gut…and then everything goes dark.

ACKNOWLEDGMENTS

Thanks be to God, above all.

I am eternally grateful to my super editor, Liz Pelletier, who is both brilliant and hilarious. Thank you for loving this book even before it deserved to be loved. Thank you to Stacy Abrams, who made me laugh continuously during her edits. I will never forget, "Is he NAKED?!?!"

Thanks to Heather Riccio for being such an amazing publicist.

Thank you to my wonderful family—Jason, Rylie, and Lainey. I am so blessed to have you. Thank you to my parents, David and Pam, who support me through this craziness called writing even when I have doubts. Thank you to my extended family and friends for loving this series and pushing for its success. I feel sure I would not be where I am in this journey without you.

Thank you to my writing friends with Entangled—Tara Fuller, Rachel Harris, Lisa Burstein, Chloe Jacobs, among others. Thank you for always offering advice and support. I feel so lucky to call you friends.

And finally, thank you to the readers and bloggers who have shown so much love and enthusiasm for this series. Your e-mails and notes are the reason I write. Thank you.

Get tangled up in our Entangled Teen titles…

Blurred *by Tara Fuller*

Cash's problems only leave him alone when he's with Anaya, Heaven's beautiful reaper. But Anya's dead, and Cash's soul resides in an expired body, making him a shadow walker, able to move between worlds. As the lines between life and death blur, Anaya and Cash find themselves falling helplessly over the edge…

Naturals *by Tiffany Truitt*

Ripped away from those she loves most, Tess is heartbroken as her small band of travelers reaches the Isolationist camp in the mysterious and barren Middlelands. Desperate to be reunited with James, the forbidden chosen one who stole her heart, she wants nothing to do with the rough Isolationists, who are without allegiance in the war between the Westerners and Easterners. But having their protection, especially for someone as powerful as Tess, may come at a cost.

Origin *by Jennifer L. Armentrout*

Daemon will do anything to get Katy back. After the successful but disastrous raid on Mount Weather, he's facing the impossible. Katy is gone. Taken. Everything becomes about finding her. Taking out anyone who stands in his way? Done. Burning down the whole world to save her? Gladly. Exposing his alien race to the world? With pleasure. Together, they can face anything. But the most dangerous foe has been there all along, and when the truths are exposed and the lies come crumbling down, which side will Daemon and Katy be standing on? And will they even be together?

Get tangled up in our Entangled Teen titles…

The Liberator *by Victoria Scott*
When Dante is given his first mission as a liberator to save the soul of seventeen-year-old Aspen, he knows he's got this. But Aspen reminds him of the rebellious life he used to live and is making it difficult to resist sinful temptations. Though Dante is committed to living clean for his girlfriend Charlie, this dude's been a playboy for far too long…and old demons die hard. Dante will have to go somewhere he never thought he'd return to in order to accomplish the impossible: save the girl he's been assigned to, and keep the girl he loves.

Everlast *by Andria Buchanan*
When Allie has the chance to work with her friends and some of the popular kids on an English project, she jumps at the chance to be noticed. And her plan would have worked out just fine…if they hadn't been sucked into a magical realm through a dusty old book of fairy tales in the middle of the library. Now, Allie and her classmates are stuck in Nerissette, a world where karma rules and your social status is determined by what you deserve. Which makes a misfit like Allie the Crown Princess, and her archrival the scullery maid.

Dear Cassie *by Lisa Burstein*
You'd think getting sent to a rehabilitation camp after being arrested on prom night would be the worst thing that happened to Cassie Wick. You'd be wrong. Chronicled in Cassie's diary over the course of her 30-day rehab, Cassie's story is one of hope, redemption, and the power of love.